THE JOONA TRILOGY ⚜ BOOK 3

The Crown of Joona

KIM V. ENGELMANN

NAVPRESS ◗

BRINGING TRUTH TO LIFE

NavPress Publishing Group

P.O. Box 35001, Colorado Springs, Colorado 80935

The Navigators is an international Christian organization. Jesus Christ gave His followers the Great Commission to go and make disciples (Matthew 28:19). The aim of The Navigators is to help fulfill that commission by multiplying laborers for Christ in every nation.

NavPress is the publishing ministry of The Navigators. NavPress publications are tools to help Christians grow. Although publications alone cannot make disciples or change lives, they can help believers learn biblical discipleship, and apply what they learn to their lives and ministries.

ISBN 08910-98674

Cover illustration: Dan Craig

The stories and characters in this book are fictitious. Any resemblance to people living or dead is coincidental.

Printed in the United States of America

1 2 3 4 5 6 7 8 9 10 11 12 13 14 15/00 99 98 97 96 95

CONTENTS

To Christopher and Julie

1
THE BRIDGE

Margaret sat up suddenly from her perch on the swinging bridge where she had been waiting since dawn.

"They're here!" she rasped to the others, who were perched along the edge of the bridge with her, legs dangling over the edge.

The moment they dreaded had finally arrived. Ryan stiffened and grasped the roped railing in front of him. Heather and Craig arched their necks to see more clearly. The trees over on the left bank were indeed crackling and swishing. Suddenly, three men in yellow hard hats emerged from the thick green woods. They had flashlights and rulers, wrenches and hammers, and loads of other weird looking tools dangling off of their belts. Their heavy work boots plopped soggy footprints into the muddy soil along the bank. The footprints began to fill up with more mud as soon as they were made.

"Thar she is, Sidney," one of the men belted out.

7

"Haven't seen one of them kinds of bridges in years. Look! Thar's a bunch of kids on it now. C'mon off of thar, ya young things! Can't tell when this thing'll fold."

"It's perfectly safe," Margaret challenged, and didn't move. "Why don't you just go away and leave us alone?"

"Well, I'll be," said another of the three men who had been addressed as Sidney. "We've got a bunch of stiff-necked children resisting this here town process."

"We'll need a stick or two of dynamite to blow up these concrete steps," said the third man, examining them carefully. He seemed gentler than the other two and more of a boss. "Sidney, Jake, go back to the truck and get some. This job shouldn't take us long. After that it's just a matter of cutting down those cables."

He looked up at the children and sighed.

"You four will need to skedaddle. This is no place for kids just now."

"I'm not moving," Margaret declared flatly.

"Neither am I," Heather announced loudly.

"Nor I," Ryan said, crossing his arms.

"Me neither," Craig added with a nasal-pitched waver to his voice.

They hadn't planned on a sitting protest. They had come early that morning to say goodbye to the bridge. Yet the brutal reality of what was about to occur stunned Margaret and she couldn't leave the bridge to its certain fate. At least not yet. If the others had consented to leaving she would have stood her ground alone. As it was, she felt strengthened by their presence.

The boss man raised his bushy eyebrows in surprise. Then he climbed the concrete steps and stood like a pillar at the end of the bridge with his hands on his hips.

"You kids, now you do as you're told. Off of this bridge or I'll have to summon your parents!"

"Our parents don't want this bridge destroyed either," Ryan countered.

"We have a town order to do this job," the boss man declared adamantly. "And we're going to do it."

Margaret couldn't have cared less if he'd had an order from Mars.

"You wouldn't want one of your friends to get hurt playing on this bridge, now would you?" the boss man tried in calmer tones. "We're here to see that no one gets hurt. Now come down easylike, and we won't have to use any force. Nice kids like you shouldn't have to be dragged."

"No one will get hurt if you just leave us alone!" Margaret shouted at him. "Come one step closer and I'll jump. I'll jump into the water and it will wash me away and I'll die. Then you'll be sorry!"

Margaret, who was still sitting with her legs dangling over the edge, moved herself out a little bit farther over the swift water as if preparing to jump. She saw the boss man back off in fright and descend the stairs warily.

"Don't jump, miss," he cautioned her, holding

up his hand. "The water is too high just now. Look, I'm leaving. I'm getting off."

Sidney and Jake returned with several sticks of dynamite under their arm and looked at their chagrined boss, puzzled.

"These kids causing you trouble, boss?" Sidney asked irritably. "'Cause if they are, we'll just summon the police. They'll lock them up and give 'em what they deserve."

"The little one with the braids is threatening to jump off," the boss man said in low tones so as not to be heard. "I don't want to be part of a child suicide. We best get some authorities in on the matter and summon the kids' parents."

Jake rolled his eyes.

"Kids these days are entirely too bratty," he mumbled with a sidelong glance up at the four children. "They think they can get away with anything. If they were mine, they'd all be in for a good thrashing."

"Well, they're not yours, Jake," the boss man retorted. "And you keep your temper. It's evident to me this bridge means a lot to these four youngsters. It's no good coaxing them. I can see that. They're bound and determined to wait us out. No, we've got to get some help down at the station."

With a last look at the children, the three men turned to leave.

"We'll be back, you young whippersnappers," Sidney yelled up at them, wagging his finger in the air. "And you're not going to like what's a comin'."

"My advice to you, children," the boss man

added, "is that you leave here before we return. It will make it easier on everyone and avoid a lot of unpleasantness."

Margaret stared unfeelingly after them as they disappeared into the woods. She hardly wanted to be thrown in prison, and she knew that once the police or whoever it was came, they could not resist any longer. Still, they had managed to buy the bridge a few more minutes of life and to her that was a victory, even if it was bittersweet.

"Thanks for staying here with me," she said to the others. "It would have been horribly lonely up here alone."

"I think we did a great job!" Craig boasted. "Why, that guy certainly didn't want to mess with you, Margaret. He really believed you were about to jump in."

"I would have, if I had too," Margaret said. "I'm a fair swimmer. I could have managed."

"And I'd have jumped in too," said Heather, and meant it.

"Me too," Ryan agreed.

"Not me," Craig whined. "I've already fallen down there, and it's no fun."

"Maybe it would have made Laurel come back," Ryan mused. "'Cause he came that first time when you fell in, Craig."

"Yeah, but that was an accident," Margaret insisted. "It's not like Laurel to be forced into something. He comes and he goes. There's no way to make him happen. You can't own him."

"I know," Ryan said wistfully. "I just thought maybe it might work . . . this once."

"I can't believe Darcy's mother," Heather said irritably. "She really is mean."

Margaret sighed and watched as Heather took a little container of apricot lip gloss out of her pocket and smeared it across her lips with her finger. Then Heather pressed her lips together and smacked them. Margaret could smell the sweet, sticky smell of the apricots from where she was sitting, even though Heather was at the opposite end of the bridge. Margaret couldn't always figure out why Heather liked the things she liked. She was so different, and yet something wonderful had happened since they had been to Joona together. Heather had become her friend. The shared experience in Joona had bonded them together with a kind of unspoken understanding that made all their differences appear trivial. It was as if at the very core they were much more alike than either of them would have dreamed possible.

"She must be the meanest sort of grownup," Margaret agreed readily. "To make such a fuss about an old bridge that's been here forever and never hurt anyone. I can't believe she got the town to agree to tear it down."

It was true. Today was the day the bridge was to be destroyed. Mary Lupus, Darcy's mother, had spearheaded the move. She had made the parents of school children concerned about its safety. It was an old bridge, she told everyone. Some of the planks were missing and its screws were rusted. It was in the thickest part of the wood and spanned the river at the widest point. Many of the children walked to and from school this way, even when their parents told them not to.

Margaret had heard rumblings about it at school and hoped against hope that it wasn't true. Perhaps it was just an ugly rumor. Perhaps it would all blow over with time. The swinging bridge was magic. How could you convince an adult of that? It was the enchanted meeting place of the great talking swan, Laurel himself. It was by the bridge that he always appeared to them. If the town destroyed it, perhaps Laurel would never return again. That's what Margaret imagined anyway as she tossed and turned in bed, night after night, worrying about what might happen. It hardly seemed fair. The bridge was Margaret's place, the only place on earth where she could go to feel close to Laurel. Sometimes on a breezy day when she visited the bridge, she could catch faint whiffs of lilac in the air. When the wind gusted and the bridge swayed back and forth, she would sit on the bridge with her legs dangling over the edge, close her eyes and feel as though she were flying high on Laurel's back again. It was a reverent, enchanted place to those who knew the secret of the great talking swan.

Uncle John, Wilda, and Bea and Casey Fitzgerald had gone to some of the meetings and tried to keep the bridge standing. Uncle John refused to sign the petition Mary Lupus had shoved in his face as he was going into the grocery store with Margaret one evening. Several more parents supported the opinion that the bridge should be left standing, since they viewed it as a historic landmark. It was a landmark, they said, that gave the town character and charm. The bridge shouldn't be destroyed just because some parents couldn't control their own children's whereabouts.

None of these arguments held any weight against the fast-talking, icy-eyed Mary Lupus, however. She was incensed that the town would even consider placing the preservation of a landmark ahead of the safety of the children. When it was suggested by Uncle John that perhaps the bridge could be repaired, he was quickly shot down. There was not enough money in the budget to do repairs. The bridge was old. It would be much less costly to simply destroy it. In the end, most of the parents joined forces with Mary Lupus. The demolition date was set for Saturday morning, May twelfth.

"I'm sorry about my mother," Darcy had told Margaret at lunch the day after the final decision was made. "I tried to stop her. I don't even know why she cares so much about it. I never walk that way to school."

Margaret just shrugged and left the table. She hadn't felt like being with Darcy on the playground that day. It was so strange that after years and years of hanging there in peace, the town should suddenly take vengeance against the bridge and want it destroyed. She had only known about the bridge for a little over two years. Why couldn't the magic of it have lasted just a little while longer?

"I asked Darcy if she wanted to come with us this morning and say goodbye," Heather mentioned, breaking into Margaret's thoughts. "But she said her mother wouldn't let her leave the house that early. Sounds like her mother's a real witch."

"She could have snuck out just the same," Margaret suggested, and then fell quiet.

The sun was getting higher in the sky and the water beneath them turning gradually from an inky black to a navy blue. The red and purple signature of dawn that had met them when they first arrived had given way to hazy sunshine.

"Remember when I threw that stupid water balloon at you?" Ryan reminisced to Margaret. "Gee whiz, was I ever immature."

"What's immachure?" asked Craig, but no one felt like offering an explanation.

"That balloon nearly killed me," Craig added with a mumble.

"It all seems like it happened ages ago," Margaret mused. "As if it were another life."

They sat in silence through the twittering birds' morning symphony and the scattered groans of the bridge as it creaked in the wind under their weight. They sat in silence as the river churned beneath them and the dew on the tall grasses along the bank was licked up by the warmth of the spring air.

"My mother came home crying last night after going out with your uncle to the movies," Ryan said finally, turning to look at Margaret. "Said your uncle was the most insensitive man she had ever known."

"You're kidding!" Margaret balked. "How could she say something like that? Uncle John thinks the world of your mom."

"It's what she said," Ryan stated somberly and shrugged. "According to her, they're not going to get married after all."

The pronouncement hung in the air like a death warrant.

"I haven't seen Uncle John yet," Margaret confessed. "I was asleep when he got home."

"Well," said Ryan thoughtfully, "Theodore has taken off again, and Mom's always kind of edgy when he's been gone all night. Maybe she's overreacting."

There was another lengthy pause in which none of them looked at each other. It was going to be a hot day. Heather removed her windbreaker.

"They haven't come back yet," Craig piped up suddenly. "The people who are supposed to tear down the bridge haven't come back. Maybe we've scared them away."

"They'll be here," Heather retorted glumly. She pulled a brush out of her tiny purse and began to run it carelessly through her hair.

"It's the good things people don't show up for," she continued, with a cynical edge to her voice. "Like volunteering for church suppers and remembering what day they're supposed to recycle their plastic. When it comes to destroying things, people always follow through, whether it's just to watch and shake their heads or to help with the process."

"That's a pretty depressing thought," Ryan countered. "I'm not sure that's always true."

"Well it's a pretty depressing day," Heather stated mildly. "My dad said yesterday that we don't have any more money and he's looking into selling the farm. He says we'll probably have to move to Kansas where our cousins live. We'll have to stay with them while my dad looks for work. My mom says we're barely breaking even with the bakery and she won't mind giving that up. The thing she'll mind is leaving all her friends here in town. My dad says the same. They grew up here."

Margaret stared at Heather.

"That's dreadful. Do you want to leave?"

"Of course not," Heather grimaced. "Especially not since I've met Laurel. I've decided that if my parents go, I'm staying here."

"You'll have to go!" Craig declared. "Dad will make you!"

"He can't make me," Heather shot back. "I'll run away."

"Where?" Craig persisted.

"I'll stay with Margaret," Heather decided suddenly. "That's okay with you, isn't it, Margaret?"

"I suppose I could hide you in the tool shed. That way Uncle John wouldn't find you."

"So there!" Heather announced triumphantly to Craig.

"Will you hide me in the tool shed too?" Craig pleaded.

"It's not very big in there," Margaret said thoughtfully. "I guess you could go in the cellar if you're very quiet. Uncle John doesn't usually go down to the cellar."

Craig looked satisfied and took a deep long breath. It was settled. They were staying.

The wind from the river blew up and gusted their faces. It was a warm wind with lots of pine smell in it. Margaret longed for it to be the fragrant pine and lilac scent she knew so well—the smell that heralded the approach of Laurel. She could not detect any lilac and her heart sank. Like Ryan, she longed for the swan to appear and call his warm greetings up to them from the river below. To fix it somehow so that the bridge wouldn't be destroyed. She looked around just to be sure she wasn't missing him, and to her joy she saw Theodore standing on the bank surveying them peacefully with a half-smile on his lips.

2

THE
MESSAGE

"Theodore!" Margaret cried. "Hi!"

Theodore waved his big white hand at them slowly and methodically.

"Hey, have you been to Joona, Theodore?" Ryan yelled down. Theodore nodded. He reached into the front pocket of his flannel shirt and pulled out a large wrinkled piece of yellowed parchment that was rolled up and ragged on the sides. It reminded Margaret of the scroll parchment the sacred text had been written on. Theodore beckoned to them with his index finger.

It seemed so odd to Margaret that Theodore should be mute when he was on earth. Actually, it didn't seem quite fair. Margaret had heard how well he spoke in Joona last time she was there. Such a great leader and spokesperson for all the swans! He knew the secrets of Joona like no one else. Perhaps that was why he was mute. Someone with a great many secrets must never be tempted to share them. Sharing too many secrets could be quite

19

dangerous. Secrets that are shared stop being secrets and too many secrets shared would put an end to all kinds of mystery about the way things are and the way things were meant to be. Margaret couldn't stand the thought of living without mystery.

"Theodore!" Margaret exclaimed, as she and the others scrambled down off the bridge. "Did you rip that paper from the sacred text?"

Theodore shook his head and unrolled the parchment carefully. Then he took his big white finger and pointed to something at the top of the parchment.

"From Milohe, Laurel, and the Rainbow," Margaret read slowly. "The following is a warning to the children who follow Laurel in the world of landbred creatures. Sent via Theodore, the executive messenger and chief informant of Joona."

"My gosh!" Heather declared. "This must be pretty important."

"It's decoded," Craig said, glancing at the parchment. "I'm glad Milohe speaks in plain English now. Those little boxes with lines running through them on that scroll were impossible!"

Theodore appeared amused and he chuckled.

"Maybe if you decode the language once," Ryan suggested thoughtfully, "there's no reason to have to decode it again. Maybe from then on you understand. You're familiar with it."

"Shall I read on?" Margaret asked humbly.

To read the letter she felt was a great honor and she didn't want to act selfish. If the others wished to read it aloud she would grant them that privilege. But they all nodded eagerly at her, even Theodore, so she cleared her voice and continued.

It has come to our attention that Sebastian's rage has exceeded all proportions of what was formerly expected. His last defeat was a great blow to his ego and he does not bear reproach well. It appears that he has decided to infiltrate earth's domain (although he has no business being there) in order that he might destroy the followers of Laurel. He feels safer on earth than in Joona, for the last victory here revealed to all the terror of his ways. He has few followers here now, although the majority on earth can still be easily deceived by him. Be on your guard, landbred creatures! You do not know when he will strike or how. The destruction of the bridge is only the first in a series of moves that might indeed become a nightmare. Do not resist those who would tear it down. It will be used eventually for our purposes. Remember that once you have recognized Sebastian is at work you have dealt your first blow, for he cannot stand to be known. We have received word that he may also have a spy on earth who is associated with you. Be vigilant. Remember that his tactics are lies, illusion, and fear. Laurel sends you his peace and assures you of his great affection. He is anxious to be with you and will appear eventually, as soon as he can.

The message ended with a smudge at the bottom of the page that looked like Theodore's thumbprint. Craig gave a low whistle after Margaret finished reading. The others just looked at each other, speechless.

"So this is Sebastian's doing!" Ryan said finally. "I never would have guessed he would try his dark magic here."

"At least we know it's him now," Margaret said, and sighed. "It doesn't sound like it's going to be easy though."

"I wonder who the spy is," Craig piped up. "Maybe its my teacher, Mrs. Jernick. She's mean."

"I hardly call giving you a note to take home when you didn't do your homework for three straight days mean," Heather commented, rolling her eyes.

"Perhaps it's Auntie Emily," suggested Margaret. "Now she's really awful."

"Whoever it is," Ryan surmised, running his fingers through his hair, "certainly won't want us to know it's them. They might not even appear mean at all. So we all have to be very careful."

Theodore nodded. He rolled the letter back up and placed it in his shirt pocket. Behind them the bridge groaned wearily for one of the last times.

"It says we're not supposed to worry about the bridge," Margaret said sadly. "I suppose there's nothing much we can do about it anyway. Even if we sat it out, they'd come and take us away by force."

"It was worth it, just to save it for a few more

minutes," Heather said. "Look at it. Isn't it the most lovely bridge in the world?"

They all paused and looked up at the bridge. It was like saying goodbye to an old friend. Its gently sloping smile had welcomed them so many times to the river. On its splintered, wooden planks they had sat and talked about so many things together as the breeze blew them from side to side, rocking them gently. It had given them a faithful pathway in the air, day after day, connecting two sides of a river that otherwise would have been impassable. Best of all, it had brought them to Laurel, and there was nothing more wonderful than that.

"I shall miss this old bridge," Craig whimpered softly.

Everyone was silent. The bridge groaned at them again as if giving a parting farewell.

"C'mon, Craig," Heather said gruffly, blinking rapidly. "It's over. We might as well go home."

Margaret followed them, wiping her eyes on her sleeve. Ryan and Theodore went off slowly in the opposite direction toward their house. There was nothing more to be said. Nothing more to be done.

At 3:20 that afternoon Margaret was lying on her bed reading. Her window was open and she heard the first blast of dynamite echo across the pale blue sky. They blasted three more times. Timidly she went and knocked on Uncle John's study door. There was a lump as big as an apple in her throat. He opened the door immediately and his face looked lined and pained. He had heard the blasting too. Uncle John crouched down and held Margaret close to him until the last rumblings died away and silence filled the room.

↬↬↬

"Uncle John," Margaret said that evening, "Ryan told me you and Wilda had a fight."

They were sitting together at the kitchen table at dinner finishing their last helping of lumpy plum pudding. Uncle John had made dinner that night and it wasn't very good. Along with the lumpy pudding he had burned the hamburgers, the mashed potatoes had the consistency of glue, and the peas were mushy. A fitting meal to a horrible day.

"I wouldn't say it was a fight," he said calmly. "We just came to terms with a few things, and it looks like it won't work out for us. That's all."

That's all! Margaret gaped at her uncle. How could he act so matter of fact when it was clear to anyone with half a brain that he was in agony. Why, Uncle John had been moping about all day. Margaret knew it was not simply the blasting of the bridge that had got him down. Why, he looked as bad as his meal tasted. His eyes were bloodshot and his mouth had a turned down scowl to it. The wrinkles in his face were so deep they seemed like little jagged cuts in his skin. Even his shoulders were stooped over more than usual.

"Well, I can't see any reason why it shouldn't work out," Margaret stated firmly with a note of irritation in her voice. "It seems to me that the two of you were made for each other."

Her uncle looked at her over a spoonful of lumpy pudding and let the spoon fall back into the bowl again. He wiped his mouth on his napkin and pushed the bowl away.

"It's not very good, is it?" he asked her sorrowfully.

Margaret shrugged. She didn't like to criticize her uncle's efforts at cooking. It was a major change for him that he cooked at all. Sometimes, at meals like this, however, Margaret secretly wished they could just eat out of cans.

"What did you fight about?" she persisted.

"Nothing that would concern you," her uncle said. Scraping his chair back against the linoleum, he got up and went to stare out the kitchen window.

"It most certainly does concern me!" Margaret declared stubbornly. "I'm a part of this thing too, as much as you are."

"You don't need to know all the details, Margaret," her uncle said soberly.

"Maybe not, but I have a right to know why you and Wilda are breaking up."

Uncle John sighed and made his way back to the chair.

"She's just not my type," he mumbled, sitting down and folding his hands on the table.

"She was until last night, Uncle John."

"All right, Margaret," her uncle said, his voice breaking slightly as he spoke. "Since you insist on knowing what it isn't necessary for you to know, I will tell you, but I do so reluctantly. I wanted to spare you the trouble. It was clear to me last night that Wilda is only dating me to fill up her time. She doesn't feel the same way about me that I do about her."

"Ryan said she cried her eyes out last night."

"That's because she felt sorry for herself. I told her straight out that I wasn't going to play games. If she wasn't serious about me, then it was time to end things here and now. That was when she left the car in a huff and slammed the door behind her."

"Well," said Margaret after a moment's pause. "I think this is Sebastian's doing, just like the bridge was. I think you should straighten things out with her as soon as you can before he makes you even more miserable."

Uncle John looked at her with shocked disbelief.

"Sebastian? You mean the dark swan, Margaret? Now you really are letting your imagination get the better of you. He doesn't have any say in this world. And what would he want with me, anyway?"

"You're a follower of Laurel aren't you?" Margaret demanded. "And I have special news—the details of which don't concern you—that indicates he is on the loose here on earth."

Uncle John's eyes were as wide as saucers.

"Margaret, you've got to be pulling my leg. There's no rhyme or reason to a deduction like that. I know you're upset about Wilda and me breaking up, but to try to manipulate me back into the relationship by throwing Sebastian into the picture is not going to work."

"I'm not manipulating!" Margaret insisted. "It's true!"

Uncle John just shook his head and stared into his bowl of lumpy plum pudding.

"This is between me and Wilda, Margaret," he said in a low voice. "Dragging you into this was a mistake. It's too upsetting. I shouldn't have even attempted a relationship with a woman. It always ends up like this."

With that he excused himself from the table and disappeared into the study, leaving Margaret alone with the dirty dishes.

The phone rang shrilly. Margaret let it ring once, twice, three times. On the fourth ring she got up to answer it. It was the last chance she had before the answering machine picked it up, and it was clear that Uncle John was ignoring it.

"Hi, Margaret?" a voice rasped over the line. "It's me, Ryan."

"Yeah," said Margaret listlessly. "What is it?"

"Have you been to see the place where the bridge was, Margaret?" he asked her. "Have you?"

"No," Margaret retorted blandly. "What's the point?"

"You ought to go and see the bridge, or rather, the place where the bridge was. You ought to go now."

"All right," Margaret conceded irritably. "I'll go. But I don't see much use to it."

"My mom's in a terrible mood," he added as an afterthought.

"Tell me about it," Margaret agreed wearily. "These grownups sure have their ups and downs don't they? It's Sebastian's doing. That's what it is."

When they hung up, Margaret left the dirty dishes and went outdoors. The blue haze of evening sifted across the sky like chalk powder. It would be dark soon. For a moment she debated whether she should even try to make it. What could possibly be at the ruins of the swinging bridge that Ryan wanted her to see? Yet she knew Ryan well enough to know he didn't make claims that weren't worthwhile. She broke into a light sprint. The air was cool and the methodical pounding of her feet against the earth somehow relieved a little of the day's tension.

The crickets were chirping early this year, for the weather had been warmer than usual. Heather had asked her yesterday if she thought catching fireflies in jars was babyish, and Margaret had said no. Then Heather had asked her if, when the fireflies came out this year, she and Margaret could catch them together in the evenings sometimes and make lanterns out of empty peanut butter jars. Margaret had agreed. She was thinking about this because she was now running through the best firefly catching area in the whole town. In the summer, for whatever reason, this section of the field near the woods was overrun with them. *It wouldn't take long to make hundreds of lanterns*, Margaret thought to herself.

The thought cheered her for a moment, but only for a moment. As she came to the edge of the woods she stopped running. The imprint of the tire tracks from the workmen's truck lay deeply pressed into the sod. Margaret had to step into the tracks to get to the path. She was overwhelmed with a deep lonely sadness as she cautiously made her way along the narrow, muddy path. She had lost a dear friend in the old bridge. How could any-thing make that right again? She didn't want to see it lying there in ruins. She didn't want to stand helplessly on one bank unable to get over to the other side. *She shouldn't have come*, she thought to herself. This was much too difficult for her to handle alone.

She almost turned around, but she was so close she decided to continue on. At least she would know what it looked like. Maybe in some odd way it would help to come back here one last time. She rounded the bend made by an overgrown blackberry bush and stopped, staring at the sight. Cables lay in stacks along the bank, and bits of concrete blown apart by the dynamite were piled neatly to one side. Margaret hardly noticed them. She stared at the river and blinked, amazed at what her eyes saw.

3
LAUREL
APPEARS

Stretched across the river where the swinging bridge had been was a brilliant rainbow. Its colors were bold and bright despite the gloom of the darkening woods. It was clear to Margaret that the rainbow had a light source all its own. The colors were just like the rainbow in Joona—gold, green, crimson, and purple. Around the rainbow the ground and the trees were lit up as if it were day and the light flashed and danced about as if it were attempting to reach out and splash the darkening landscape with brilliant color.

Margaret hadn't looked at the rainbow for very long when she saw something flickering white out of the corner of her left eye. Across the river, on the opposite bank, his feathers radiant in the light, stood Laurel. His eyes shone as if there were tiny flames behind them. He bent down low to greet her in a swan smile.

"Laurel!" Margaret cried, running to the edge of the river. "Laurel! How do I get across to come to you? They took down the bridge, Laurel. Did you know? Of course you know! You told us in the letter. How do I reach you, Laurel? The water is too high and . . ."

"Peace, Margaret," Laurel interrupted her softly. "I have come to assure you of my presence, and to strengthen you for the time ahead. It is much harder for you to cross over to me, so if you wouldn't mind, I shall simply cross over to you."

Margaret nodded eagerly and stepped into the circle of light made by the rainbow so she could watch the swan more clearly. With gentle grace Laurel opened his wide white wings and flew over the surging river in a moment. He landed in the circle of light near Margaret and folded his wings neatly across his back. The colors from the rainbow flickered and danced off Laurel's white feathery sheen making it seem as if the swan were arrayed with countless sparkling jewels. Laurel reached out his long neck to nuzzle Margaret with his beak, but she was already flinging herself at him, embracing his torso and reaching up to kiss his small bony cheek.

"I have missed you, Laurel," Margaret cried. "I've missed you more this time than even I did last time, although the last time you left I thought at times I would die without you."

Laurel extended his wings and wrapped Margaret up in them. It was the same kind of warm, downy embrace he always gave her. The kind of embrace Margaret tried to recapture in her thoughts again and again, especially on cold winter nights when the heat wasn't turned up high enough and she would wake up stiff and shivering under her blankets. Not only were Laurel's feathers warm, but they were comforting, easing every last bit of fear out of her.

"Margaret," Laurel crooned, "are you able to come with me tonight?"

"Of course I can come," Margaret said, looking into the swan's soft gaze. "Where are you taking me?"

"High above the earth to Joona," Laurel told her, and when he spoke the scent of pine and lilac filled the air. "Sebastian cannot hear us there. He has begun his warfare on earth now, and who knows but that he may be listening to us now. We musn't chance being overheard."

"Oh Laurel," Margaret said, sighing with relief. "I was hoping you might say that. I could use a good dose of Joona about now. It has been so dreadfully depressing here."

"Look at the rainbow, Margaret," Laurel said reverently. "It will not normally be visible to you. I have shown it to you now so that you will remember something very important in the days ahead."

"What is it?" Margaret asked solemnly.

She took a deep breath trying to absorb as much of the beauty of the sparkling light as possible.

"No matter how difficult things appear," Laurel told her, "you must remember that an invisible rainbow looms at the places of Sebastian's destruction. Right now the rainbow stretches where the old swinging bridge once hung. It is a sign, a promise from Milohe, the Source of all promises and expectations."

"You mean," asked Margaret longingly, "that the swinging bridge might come back some day?"

"Perhaps," Laurel said, fluffing his feathers. "Although you can't know in specific language like that. You just have to trust that the promise is good."

"Oh," said Margaret. "I see, although I wish I knew."

"If you knew everything," Laurel said simply, "you would have no room for trust or surprise, or even laughter, since you usually laugh when something takes a slightly different turn than what you expect."

"Mystery," breathed Margaret softly. "That's the most amazing truth of all, isn't it?"

"To be sure," Laurel agreed.

"My back is reserved for you alone tonight," the swan declared, after they had stood for a few moments looking silently at the rainbow. "Climb aboard and we shall ride the breeze the way it was meant to be ridden! We shall soar and plummet our way to the paradise of swans on the swift currents of air that weave their way through the loom of the night sky. You might say, we shall have a current event! Yes, it shall be just you and me tonight, Margaret. The wind is calling and I have bounce in my wings. Besides, it is much more pleasant to dance in the night sky when one has an experienced riding companion such as yourself for company."

Margaret eagerly shinnied up the wing he held out for her. Plopping down onto Laurel's back, she sank deep into his feathers that were still twinkling with flecks of colored light from the rainbow. They took off as easily as if they were riding a smooth, capped wave that curved forever upward into the sky.

As soon as they left the shining circle of light created by the rainbow they were enveloped in dusky blue darkness. Margaret's hair flew back from her face and she felt the familiar friendly gusts brush her cheeks with enthusiastic strokes. She reached her arms up over her head like she did when she was on the Great Dragon, the biggest, tallest roller coaster in the area. It was the kind of roller coaster that went upside-down in the middle of the ride and made your stomach flip-flop. Just as she was remembering the sensation, Laurel stopped flapping and seemed to pivot in the air. Then with a wild rush downward he sailed, head first, straight for the earth. Margaret screamed as she always did when she rode the Great Dragon, and she clutched at Laurel's neck. Just when she thought they'd hit the earth for sure, Laurel somersaulted. Margaret's head flew backwards and she watched for a split second as the sky seemed to rotate around her. Then they were soaring up again like a rocket, as fast as they had soared down, banking, diving, and occasionally flipping around again in backward somersault dives.

Tonight Laurel hardly paused between his acrobatic moves. It was the most exhilarating ride Margaret had ever taken on the swan and she could scarcely catch her breath. She was astounded at the swan's energy and grace. He never seemed to tire, gliding from one move to the next as if performing a great ballet in which he was the only dancer.

"Isn't the night air glorious?" Laurel yelled back to her. "It's full of play and bounce tonight."

"Do keep going, Laurel!" Margaret called back breathlessly. "I've never had so much fun!"

"A bit more then!" the swan conceded cheerily.

The wind caught them again and they hurtled through the air at a dizzying pace. Swooping downward Laurel paused, letting the air currents carry them upward again in a wide, arching spiral that spun them slowly and evenly away from the ground. They climbed higher and higher as Laurel gave himself to the wind, holding his wings motionless as a statue. Looking up, Margaret saw the full yellow moon staring at her with its shadowy craters that looked like the vacuous eyes of a skull. The stars were out tonight as well playing peekaboo with the dark shadows of clouds as they rapidly paraded across the sky in the exuberant energy of the wind.

"We must be off now," Laurel said finally after one last plummet. "I want to take you to the sacred room in Joóna. It has a fountain of royal water in it and a large, stained-glass window. It is in the left wing, or should I say left pinion of the castle. Have you been there, Margaret?"

"No, but I think Ryan told me about it," Margaret said, after thinking for a moment. "I believe he came across the room when he invaded the castle last time we were there. He said it had some sort of poem written on a plaque in the wall."

"A poem, yes," mused the swan. "A prophetic poem to be precise. Otherwise known as the Rhyme of the Royalty. Do you know what the words are, Margaret?"

"No," Margaret confessed. "Ryan tried to remember, but he couldn't."

"It is of great importance that you commit the words to memory," Laurel told her. "The words have power and will strengthen you for what lies ahead. Only those of royal heritage are able to remember the rhyme."

"And am I?" Margaret gasped. "Am I of royal . . . what was it . . . heritage?"

"Anyone who is princess of Joona must have royal blood in them," Laurel said with great solemnity in his voice. "And you are princess, are you not? Clearly your mother, but also your father are of such royal stock as well."

"What on earth are you talking about?" Margaret countered.

After she said it, Margaret realized they weren't on earth at all and that maybe the expression had been a bit inappropriate. Things were different when you were hurtling through the night sky. Very different. Things were different when you were in Joona, too. Still, the phrase, "What in sky are you talking about?" didn't sound right either.

The swan was silent, so Margaret cleared her throat.

"My father was just a dumb old drunk," she announced bitterly. "He was as mean as tacks."

"Quite to the contrary," Laurel retorted. "You never actually met your father, Margaret."

They were almost to where the mountains began and it was getting so windy that the swan had to slow his pace a little. Margaret sat bolt upright on Laurel's back, the wind battering her face, and wondered if she were hearing correctly. Perhaps the wind had distorted what she thought she heard Laurel just say.

"Of course I met him!" she yelled into the howling gusts. "He was always drunk—that's what I remember. He fell into a canal one time after he left us when I was only six and drowned. I didn't even miss him. I just pretend I never had a father. I don't think about him and I never hardly ever talk about him."

The swan was quiet for a few moments flapping forcefully against the heavy winds. Margaret thought perhaps she had told Laurel something he hadn't known before.

"The man you are describing," Laurel finally yelled back to her, "is not the one of whom I speak.

The man you are describing is certainly not your father."

Margaret's mouth fell open. It was too windy to do any more talking in the sky. She saw the clearing beneath them and her ears crackled and popped as they made a rather bumpy descent.

"How . . . how can it be true?" she bumbled, as the swan hit the soft, bouncy turf and took a few running strides forward.

It was quieter now, the trees providing a welcome breaker to the wind's incessant howling.

"My mother never told me," she added with puzzled uncertainty. "Why wouldn't she have said something?"

"She wanted to," Laurel said softly. "It wasn't like your mother to ever hide the truth from you, but she was waiting for you to get a bit older. She wanted you to be able to understand."

"Understand what?" Margaret demanded.

"The complexities of love," Laurel said with an amused lilt to his voice. "She didn't want you to think less of her, Margaret, because of what had happened before."

"What do you mean, Laurel? What happened before?"

"Perhaps it would be best to wait," the swan suggested gently. "Until we reach the sacred room. There your mother wishes to meet you and tell you herself."

"She does?"

"She is waiting for you eagerly," Laurel assured her.

Margaret descended Laurel's back and ran to unlock the stone door. As she mounted Laurel's back again and they began to fly rapidly over the surging river through the cave, she could hardly keep from smiling. An immense weight she hadn't known she'd been carrying with her all these years had been lifted off her shoulders. Everything she saw around her seemed more distinct and clear— the transparent beauty of the sparkling waterfall as they flew over the quiet pool and the wet, glistening texture of the cave walls that made the rock look like polished black diamonds winking like stars; the white frothy texture of the water tumbling through the cave beneath them and the gentle spray from the foam that lightly coated her face with cool, sweet Joona water. It all made Margaret want to dance inside. To think that her real father might have been someone who was in love with her mother, who cared for them, who was perhaps kind and wise was more than she could fathom. Yet it was true. Laurel had said so, and she knew so deep inside.

"It's enchanted in here," Margaret breathed, barely audibly. "Magical. It's like I'm seeing it all for the very first time."

"Perhaps you are," Laurel declared, and Margaret was surprised that he had heard her. "It's amazing what can happen when you shake a little weight off your tail feathers. You don't just fly, you soar!"

As Laurel said this they burst into the dazzling light of Joona's rainbow. Margaret gasped. The colors were brilliantly toned and alive with movement. They flew through each band of the rainbow rapidly, the light from each band changing everything, even Margaret's skin, to that same color—purple, gold, crimson, and green. She heard Joona music playing and off in the distance the singing of swans.

"They always sing now," Laurel said, cocking his head toward the sweet medley of voices that floated toward them. "Ever since you and the others freed Joona from the cruel pinions of the Regalia. If they knew you were here just now the swans would never let you leave, and we haven't time to stay for long. We must go directly to the castle. There will be a time, Margaret, when you shall stay here for as long as you wish, and when the crown of Joona will be yours to wear."

"When will that be?" Margaret asked, wishing Laurel would decide to let her stay forever right now.

"After you have brought Joona to earth," Laurel said simply, and banked to the far left, circling in the sky toward the castle.

Margaret didn't understand what he was talking about, but she often didn't. Looking up she saw that the castle was nearly upon them and that it looked friendly and homey, with its wide gray columns and spearlike spires reaching for the sky. She remembered how dismal and dark the castle had looked when the Regalia had it in their possession. This castle seemed almost like a different building altogether. It was odd the way buildings sometimes took on the atmosphere of the creatures living inside.

For a moment it looked as though Laurel was about to fly directly into the castle's stone pillar. Then, without warning, he swooped downward and they shot through an open window Margaret hadn't seen from the air. She knew as soon as they entered the castle that they were in the sacred room, the room Ryan had described to her. Laurel landed gracefully on the inlaid tile that surrounded a tall pristine fountain. The tile was shiny, and after getting off Laurel's back, Margaret reached down to touch it. It was smooth and glossy and laid out to show the pattern of purple lilacs. Standing up, she surveyed the fountain. It was large and made of white marble. The water shooting up from the center was full of color. It shot up almost as high as the castle ceiling and then curved over in the air, splashing down on three marble tiers below. Beyond the fountain, Margaret could see a wall made of stained glass through which the sun was shining. Slowly she walked over to it and saw it just the way Ryan had described. The window depicted an enormous white swan who was soaring through the sky over a tiny ball that seemed to be earth.

"Is this you, Laurel?" Margaret asked quietly.

The room was not a place you were supposed to talk very loudly. Margaret could tell that by the hush in the air.

"Yes," Laurel said, coming to stand next to her. "It was fashioned from Joona water and sand and put there to remind the suffering swans that whether they reside on earth, in Joona, or in the heavens, I am always there for them. You'd think they wouldn't need a window to remind them of such an obvious thing, but it seems to assist them when they are in need of inspiration."

"It's beautiful," Margaret breathed.

"Here is the poem you referred to before," Laurel said, stepping over to a stone that jutted out of the wall a bit and was next to the heavy wood door.

"It's carved into the rock, Margaret," Laurel continued with a certain majesty in his voice. "Milohe wrote it with his own finger many eons ago. It would do you well to commit it to memory since it will give you strength on earth for the days ahead."

As soon as he said this, Laurel opened his wings and trumpeted. It sounded off the stone walls of the castle with a mellow richness and vibrated in the air like the pulsing of Margaret's own heart. She knew it was a call—her call—to fight Sebastian, but somehow the quality of Laurel's trumpeting told her she would not have to fight in the same way she had fought before. The trumpet of the swan was wistful and melancholic, as if it were able to plumb the depths of brokenness and pain. It was not the frisky, spirited march he had used before when they had infiltrated the castle and used their stars.

Margaret walked over to Laurel and stared at

the poem in the stone. The letters were worn with the years and she could tell they were not as deep as they once had been. Still, as she mouthed the words silently, they gave her a deep peace and she felt suddenly, strangely confident.

Uprisings of power will shake the kingdom
Our lives will be put to the test
For those alone without a friend
There will be no rest
Yet in the midst of dark despair
Where life is nearly death
Laurel who plummets the sulfur sea
Will awaken in us a victory.

"I think I've got it," Margaret said after about five minutes of reading the words again and again.

She wanted not only to memorize the poem but to let the words sink down inside her so that she wouldn't forget them, even if she were in the middle of a crisis. As Margaret whirled around to face Laurel she not only saw the swan, but beyond Laurel she saw her mother on the tiles by the fountain draped in a golden shawl that reached all the way to her feet. On her head she wore a wreath of vines identical to the one the swans had made for Margaret. She was smiling, and her hair was loose and wavy like a waterfall.

"Greetings, my dear!" her mother called out to her. "Come to me so that I can look at you. Are you well, Margaret?"

Margaret ran and embraced her mother. Her mother smelled of lilacs.

"I was out walking in the gardens of Joona," her mother said, after they had hugged for a very long time. "Waiting for you to come seemed like waiting for eternity to end."

She led Margaret to a little bench and they sat down by the sparkling fountain. Laurel joined them. He nestled up on his belly near Margaret's feet and placed his head in her lap. Margaret stroked Laurel's head gently and felt joy rising in her higher than the fountain itself. She was always surprised at how beautiful her mother was. Far more beautiful than she remembered her being on earth. It must be that her mother looked now much the way she was meant to be.

"I am afraid we don't have much time," her mother told her. "I shall have to be quick about this. Joona time and earth time don't match up too well."

"Our dancing in the night air went a little longer than expected," Laurel said with a slight chuckle. "It is so wonderfully uplifting to join the wind in its escapades. Margaret is an excellent rider. Many would have been blown away by such a thrill."

"It was wonderful!" exclaimed Margaret. "We even did somersaults."

"Plummeting right for the ground first, I suspect," her mother said, and laughed. "How well I remember my first somersault on Laurel. I was sure we were going to crash. Laurel, you have a knack for waiting until the last second to display your artistry."

"It's all in resting in the wind," Laurel said, and sighed as if reliving the celestial experience.

"So I shall be quick about this, darling," her mother intoned to Margaret. "I can't wait until you will come and be with us for a longer time. Your crown rests in my quarters locked in a clear glass case, and I long for you to wear it and rule with me here. It is a glorious land as you know, full of rainbow music and song, lilacs and pine, crystal water and soaring swans. There is only one more thing you must do first. It comes to all of royal distinction. It is in our blood to want liberty for the creatures who inhabit the planets on which we live. It is only natural to want this when you are of ruling caliber. So, my child, you must endure what will be difficult for you on the shadowy regions of earth. I cannot tell you all that lies in store, but you must never despair. Like the picture in the stained glass, you must remember Laurel's presence with you always, even when you feel alone."

"I shall," promised Margaret, nodding solemnly.

"And although you may be upset with me, I shall need to tell you something else," her mother continued, looking down. "It is true what Laurel told you about your father, Margaret. The man you remember, my darling, was a poor substitute for the man I loved. A poor substitute for the man who gave you to me."

Suddenly Margaret's eyes were swimming with

tears. She nodded and didn't say anything. She couldn't say anything. Margaret's mother cleared her throat.

"His name was Grant, Margaret. Uncle John was the only one who knew we actually married. Both of our sets of parents were a bit strict and old-fashioned at times, or so we thought. We had been going out for a couple of years and decided we didn't want to put up with the big, stuffy wedding they wanted us to have. It was crazy what we did. We ran away and got married one rainy night in the middle of June. Three nights we were gone. Grant was a military man and worked for the special forces. When we returned he got a telephone call. He was to leave for a small island in the Atlantic the next day for an undetermined period of time. That was the last time I saw your father, Margaret. He was shot overseas, and I was heartbroken."

"Oh," said Margaret, blinking back her tears.

There was a long pause in which no one said anything, and the only sound was the bubbling of the fountain as it splashed down over the three-tiered marble base.

"How come you didn't tell me before?"

"I'm sorry, Margaret," her mother said, reaching over to grasp her hand. "I married Lyman a few months later out of silly pressure from my friends and to fill the gaping loneliness I felt. It was stupid, but I did it. I told him about my marriage to Grant and that I was pregnant, and he made me promise never to tell a soul. He wanted you to be his child, and I consented at the time not knowing what a tyrant he would turn out to be. When you were born, Margaret, I looked into your little eyes and saw Grant staring back at me. You are so like him, my dear. I knew I had to tell you one day. I didn't want you to know too early, lest you take my impulsiveness and irresponsibility to heart and follow my poor example in your own life."

"You're not impulsive and irresponsible," Margaret said, wiping her tears away with the back of her hand. "You're wonderful."

"Love does strange things to people, Margaret," Laurel chimed in. "You shall see for yourself in a few years."

"I'm never going to fall in love," Margaret retorted. "So you don't have to worry about me."

Margaret's mother smiled, amused.

"There's a picture, Margaret," she said.

"A picture of what?" Margaret asked. "You mean of my father?"

"Yes dear," her mother said gently. "Ask Uncle John if he can find it for you. I seem to remember putting it somewhere very special. He may remember where."

"And now, Margaret," Laurel whispered in her ear. "Drink of the water in the fountain. It is Joona water, yes, but it is even more powerful, for it has been purified ten times beyond. That is because it has circled Milohe's throne and come here after being seared with his light. It will get into your system and strengthen you for what lies ahead. A golden cup is on the rim of the third tier. Take it and drink."

Walking over to the fountain, Margaret found the cup at once. It was hanging from a small brass hook and had a jeweled handle. She held the cup under the liquid color that came gushing down over the tiers and watched as it filled up her little cup in seconds. Strangely, steam billowed over the sides of the cup as if she were holding something very hot. The water, however, had been cool to her touch and as she placed the rim to her lips it also was cool.

Margaret took a sip and felt the water's energy buzz through her insides like an electric current. Although it was cool when she drank it, it was hot inside her afterward, and she could drink only three cups of it before she felt as though her insides were ready to boil over.

"It is enough," Laurel told her kindly. "You are well equipped."

"Tell me what will happen, Laurel," Margaret pleaded, feeling as though she were going to faint as the heat from the liquid bubbled within her. "It is so awful not to know."

"It will be bearable, and it will be of your own choosing, Margaret," Laurel told her. "Milohe, in his wisdom, does not force these things on anyone. They come as a natural consequence of one's compassion for another. It is most essential that you proceed in peace, not in fear."

"One more item of essential importance, my

dear," Margaret's mother told her, holding out her hand in invitation for Margaret to resume her place next to her on the bench. "It may be encouraging to you."

Margaret came and sat down. She was still feeling dizzy from the water and was glad to get off her feet.

"Although I can't spell it out in detail, the next few days you spend on earth will be essential if we are to find your father."

The words rang in Margaret's ears like a buzzer. She heard them but couldn't make sense of them.

"Find my father?" she repeated dreamily. "What do you . . . oh my! I feel so very off balance."

"It's the water," she heard Laurel say somewhere far, far away.

The swan was by her side and put his wing around her shoulder.

"This sometimes happens when too much of this water is drunk too rapidly. I do apologize for the inconvenience, but the side effects will wear off shortly. I should have warned you of its potency. Lean on my wing; better yet, see if you can climb aboard. You are welcome to lie down in my feathers."

"But . . ." Margaret stammered, trying to stand.

Her mother held her other arm to help her onto Laurel's back. The room was spinning around. Margaret fought to keep awake. She wanted to know what her mother meant when she said the part about finding her father. In her foggy state of mind she couldn't form the words to ask any more questions. She fought the dizziness, but it was overpowering. Her mother called goodbye and then she heard the familiar flapping of Laurel's wings. They were airborne, and Margaret let the dizziness have her. Nestling deep into the down, her head against the back of Laurel's smooth, serpentine neck, Margaret fell asleep.

She woke up later that night and found herself back in her own bed with the quilt tucked up around her chin. She felt a certain fluttery excitement in her chest that she hadn't felt before, almost as if Laurel were enfolding her heart with his gigantic pearl-white wings.

"It's a pity," Margaret thought to herself groggily, "that you can't always see a rainbow on earth like you can in Joona. It might make us all a bit happier from one day to the next. It's hard to imagine invisible rainbows, although for Laurel's sake I shall have to try."

A blast of thunder followed by a zag of lightning jolted Margaret wide awake. She suddenly realized that her bedroom window was open and rain was soaking her rug. She got out of bed and bolted the window closed. The house creaked and rattled in the storm like an old car trying to start its engine. Margaret was sure the roof was about to fly off and be ripped to shreds as the winds pounded their howling beat against the sagging walls of the old house. Grabbing the quilt off her bed and putting it around her shoulders, she tiptoed into the hall. She was startled to see Uncle John standing in the corridor. He had on striped pajamas and was staring straight ahead as if he were in a trance. He seemed not even to see her.

"Uncle John," Margaret whispered, pulling on his sleeve. "Are you all right?"

"I had a dream," he mumbled almost incoherantly. "It was about Sebastian. There's something weird going on around here, Margaret. Something very weird, and I don't like it one bit."

"What was the dream about?" Margaret asked, feeling a tremor go down her spine. "I've got to know."

4
THE
PHOTOGRAPH

Uncle John shook his head back and forth a few times and stretched his eyes open very wide.

"Goodness," he exclaimed, rubbing his hand across his face so that his drooping wrinkles sagged all the more, "I feel like I'm six years old again and scared of the dark. C'mon, Margaret. Let's go down and get some milk."

Margaret followed him to the kitchen and sat in a chair backwards watching while Uncle John rummaged in the refrigerator to see if there was any chocolate sauce. When he found some he decided to make cocoa. He poured some milk in a pan and put it on the stove. Then he came over and sat down next to Margaret.

"Warm milk and chocolate sauce always made me happy when I was a kid," he said smiling wearily. "Hopefully it will do the same thing now."

"Well?" asked Margaret pointedly.

"Well what?" asked her uncle, looking at her with bloodshot eyes.

"The dream, Uncle John," Margaret said, her voice edged with frustration. "What was the dream about?"

Uncle John just frowned and shook his head slowly.

"I'm not sure," he said, looking troubled. "All I know is the feeling I got from it. To put it bluntly, I woke up in pure terror and my sheets were drenched in sweat. My pajamas are sticking to me like glue. I know one thing I didn't know before. He's here, all right, just like you said. Sebastian is here, and he's angry. There's no telling what he might do, Margaret. You and I must be very careful."

"I know," said Margaret solemnly. "It hasn't been easy lately. You've got to talk to Wilda, Uncle John. You've got to make things right again."

"Yes, yes of course," Uncle John said, nodding his head slightly. "It must be the right time though. I don't want to push myself on her."

"She's probably dying to hear from you," Margaret advised him gently.

"Do you think so, Margaret?"

"I know so," Margaret assured him.

Uncle John got up and poured the steaming milk into two mugs. He squirted a few globs of chocolate sauce into each one and stirred them noisily.

"Let's go into the living room," he suggested. "It's drafty in here."

They left the kitchen and went into the next room. Uncle John flicked on a brass lamp sitting on an end table and lowered himself into the wicker rocking chair. Margaret took her place in the corner of the couch and kicked off her slippers. The place where they were sitting was golden in the light but the shadows in the recesses of the room seemed deep and ominous.

"Margaret," Uncle John said to her seriously. The lines in his face lengthened until they ran into each other. "Where did you go this evening?"

Margaret gulped. She wasn't sure she should say anything. She wasn't supposed to go out after dark. She looked around, trying to think of something to say. The shadows in the room seemed as if they might be hiding creatures of all shapes and sizes. Creatures with open mouths who would swallow Margaret up into their cavernous insides. Uncle John cleared his throat, waiting.

"I went for a walk," Margaret said suddenly. "I was sort of upset, you know, about everything."

Her uncle took a sip of his milk.

"Margaret, you must learn to tell me when you leave the house. I was quite concerned. Darcy stopped by when you were gone. She wanted to talk to you. She seemed upset."

"She did?" Margaret asked, surprised.

She and Darcy hadn't been spending much time together lately, ever since Darcy's mom had started promoting the destruction of the swinging bridge.

"Yes," Uncle John said soberly. "When I couldn't

55

find you, I told her to come back in the morning. I waited up for you quite some time, and when you didn't come I went to bed. You must have come in just after that, because an hour later I checked your room and you were all tucked in and the window was wide open. I didn't close it. I thought you might have wanted the air, although at that time it wasn't raining."

"Oh," said Margaret again, looking up at her uncle as innocently as she knew how. "I closed it just now."

Her uncle had that sound to his voice he always had when he was about ready to punish her. She should just tell him that Laurel had taken her away and given her the thrill of her life on the wind. She should let him know that she had seen her mother and drunk from the fountain that ran by Milohe's throne. Suddenly a thought hit her, but not soon enough.

"I am going to have to ground you for the weekend, Margaret," Uncle John was saying. "You can't go running around without letting me know where you are. It's much too dangerous, especially right now."

"Actually," Margaret said cautiously, "I was with Laurel. I know about my father, Uncle John. My mother told me about Grant tonight."

Uncle John looked at her. His mouth fell open and his mug nearly dropped out of his hand.

"Your cocoa, Uncle John," Margaret said,

motioning to her uncle's mug. "You're tilting your cocoa and it's about ready to slop onto the floor."

"Oh my," said Uncle John, bringing his mug upright and trying to regain his composure.

"My mother said there was a photo," Margaret continued in a matter-of-fact way. "Of my real father, that is. She said she hid it somewhere special and thought you might remember where."

A smile crept across John's face.

"I was getting ready to tell you one of these days," he said quietly. "I didn't quite know how to begin, but I knew she'd want you to know. I guess I waited too long and she finally took matters into her own hands. You can go where you want this weekend. I didn't understand. Come with me now, Margaret."

Uncle John stood up and reached for her hand. He led Margaret into the dark study and flicked on the light. Margaret could hear the wind howling viciously and the windows chattering as they banged back and forth in their loose metal frames. This part of the house was the original structure, and if anything was going to blow apart tonight, Margaret was sure it would be this room. She watched Uncle John rummaging through his bookshelves. He had all sorts of dull kinds of books in his study—which, for some reason Margaret could not figure out, he dearly loved. There were books on biology, chemistry, and anatomy in one section. In another section he had medical journals arranged by date, some going back as far as 1957. Margaret figured that was when people lived without electricity. Another section had less ominous sorts of reading, such as "How to Fly Fish in Ten Easy Steps," or "A Homeowner's Guide to Repairs." Still, another section had a potpourri of items that didn't seem to fit anywhere—things like a wooden carving of a pelican on a rock, odd sculptured bookends, a tiny globe, old newspapers, a tape recorder, and some dried out magic markers.

Here it was that Uncle John rummaged. He looked only for a few moments before retrieving an old, faded scrapbook. Margaret knew that scrapbook. It had been her mother's. It had a pencil sketch of Laurel in it drawn by her mother when just a little girl. Uncle John had told her once that her mother had drawn that picture right after meeting Laurel for the first time. Margaret loved that picture of Laurel with his neck bent down low in a swan smile. It looked so much like him. Many times, on rainy afternoons, she had opened the scrapbook just to browse. There were leaves pressed in waxed paper, dried, crumbling flowers, old photographs with yellowed tape across the corners, and poems and stories her mother had composed. Margaret never tired of going through it.

Now she watched as her uncle carefully creaked open the leather binding of the scrapbook and slowly thumbed through the thick pages. Margaret knew there wasn't anything in that scrapbook she hadn't seen a thousand times already.

"I don't think the picture would be in there," she

said, looking over John's shoulder as he lowered himself into an easy chair. "I know that book inside and out."

Uncle John just smiled at her and continued to flip the pages over with great care. When he reached the picture of Laurel, he stopped. It was taped into the book across each corner and along each side. Uncle John gently removed one of the long pieces of tape. It came off easily enough, being old and crackly. Then, to her surpise, her uncle reached in behind the picture.

"Yes," John said, still with a half-smile on his face. "I thought I remembered her doing this."

Carefully he pulled out a small white envelope with some writing on the back.

"It says, 'Grant and Annie on their wedding day.'"

He handed the envelope to Margaret.

"Take a look at your parents, Margaret."

Margaret's hands trembled as she took the envelope. She went and sat down in the rocking chair. The envelope was sealed and she fumbled with it for a few seconds before succesfully breaking it open. Her hand shook as she reached for the photograph inside. She could barely grasp it at first. It was a black and white photograph with a bumpy wrinkle through the center of it, but Margaret hardly noticed. Her eyes were fixed on the man who held her mother's arm in his. The man's whole face was smiling. His eyes were bright, his mouth grinning, and even his moustache had a lively upward twist to it at the ends. He was a handsome man, despite the fact that he was a few inches shorter than Margaret's mother. Margaret thought he looked as though he would have made a wonderful father. His hair was very short, military style, and he was dressed in a beige uniform with stripes on the lapel. Margaret looked at her mother. She was smiling and her whole face was radiant. Her hair was loose, cascading down around her shoulders. She wore a flowered dress and held a yellow rose in one hand.

"It's the only picture they had taken of their wedding," Uncle John said softly after Margaret had stared at it for a long while. "What do you say we go and buy a proper frame for it tomorrow and hang it in your room?"

Margaret nodded without taking her eyes off the photograph.

"I saw your mother hide it," Uncle John told her, "on the day she found out about Grant's death. She didn't know I saw her do it. She told me later that her two greatest loves were on page seventeen of her scrapbook. I wouldn't have known what she meant if I hadn't seen her stuff the photo behind Laurel's drawing."

"Her two great loves, Laurel and my father," Margaret said nodding, her eyes misty. "He looks like he was such a nice man."

"Great sense of humor, soft-spoken, gentle as a lamb," Uncle John said, shaking his head remembering. "And he had the courage of a lion. Had

medals all over his room for one or another courageous mission he had accomplished. Annie took
me there once."

"Did he like children?" Margaret asked
cautiously.

"Taught Sunday school to third graders for all
the years I knew him," Uncle John said wryly.
"Loved kids. Even helped coach the softball team
when the school needed volunteers."

"I wish he'd known me," Margaret said wistfully.
"I wish it with all my heart."

"You would have been his pride and joy,
Margaret," Uncle John said. "I can guarantee you
of that."

Margaret looked down at the photograph and
became absorbed in it again. The silence was bro-
ken by the high-pitched ringing of the phone on her
uncle's desk. Margaret jerked upright and stared
at her uncle in bewilderment. Who on earth would
be calling so late?

"Probably the hospital," Uncle John said
wearily, getting to his feet. "This happens every now
and then, but they're supposed to call my beeper
first. At least I'm awake this time."

He picked up the receiver.

"Hello? Ryan? What in blazes are you doing calling this time of night?"

There was a pause in which Margaret watched
her uncle's face grow ashen white.

"Don't move her, Ryan," he said sternly. "I'm calling an ambulance immediately to go to your house

and get your mom. I'll meet her at the hospital. No . . . no, you did the right thing to call. Sit tight now, and help will be on its way. Don't worry."

Uncle John didn't even look up at Margaret as he quickly jabbed seven more numbers into the telephone.

"Hello, Kurt? This is John Morrison. I need an ambulance over at 14 Ballantine Avenue ASAP. The woman is breathing but is unconscious, according to her son. I'll meet you at the hospital."

Uncle John dashed out of the study and up the stairs to change clothes. In less than a minute, he was out the front door and Margaret heard the Jeep roar away, its tires squealing on the pavement. Margaret's heart pounded in her chest. She looked at the clock. It was 2:15.

She walked over to the phone and dialed Ryan's number. The phone rang only once before Ryan's quavering voice answered.

"Hello?"

"Hello, Ryan? It's Margaret. What's going on?"

"It's my mom, Margaret. I heard her scream and when I went into her room she was lying on the floor moaning. I can't wake her up though. She's had this really bad cough for a long time but she thought it was just the flu. I bet its pneumonia or something."

"She's breathing, right?" Margaret asked.

"Yeah, but her lips are bluish. She's right here next to me. I don't know what to do. . . . "

Ryan's voice trailed off.

"Ryan, Uncle John has called an ambulance.

They'll be there in a few minutes. Just try to relax. Where's Theodore?"

"He's here with me," Ryan told her shakily. "He heard her scream too and came in when I did."

"Ryan! It's Sebastian! It has to be!" Margaret exclaimed. "I've been with Laurel tonight and he warned me that things like this would start happening. This is Sebastian's revenge, Ryan. Send Theodore to Joona tomorrow so he can keep Laurel posted about what's going on. We'll need all the help we can get."

Margaret felt the warmth of the water she had drunk from the fountain bubbling up on her insides. For a moment she felt very strong. "I'm here for you, Ryan," she said calmly. "Whatever you need, just call me."

"I'll tell Theodore," Ryan said softly. "They're at the door. I've got to go."

Ryan hung up, and Margaret paced restlessly around the study for a while. Finally she went back upstairs and crawled into bed. The rain was still battering at her window. She propped the picture of her father and mother against the lamp on her bedside table and lay staring at it in the light from the hall. She had left the door ajar in case the phone might ring. For what seemed like an eternity she lay there with her eyes wide open.

Things were happening quickly and her mind was reeling. She knew she had to stay calm, think clearly, and be on her guard. Still, despite the assurances Laurel had given her and the bubbling of the water deep inside her, fear clutched at her throat and it hurt to swallow. Her father was smiling at her in the dim light. It was almost as if he were telling her that he loved her.

She must have fallen asleep, for she was suddenly jolted awake by the telephone's ring. Dawn was just etching its gray-blue streaks across the sky and the birds were beginning to sing. Margaret raced downstairs to the kitchen phone and almost slipped on the throw rug in the hall.

"Hello?" she rasped into the telephone.

"Hi, Margaret, it's me, Ryan. I'm at the hospital. They let me ride here in the ambulance."

"How's your mom?"

"Uncle John is with her. She's in ICU. They won't let me in just now. They're working on her."

"What's ICU?"

"Intensive Care Unit. For people who are really sicker than sick."

"Oh Ryan!" Margaret groaned.

"It's pneumonia," Ryan said softly, "and Mom's in a coma from it."

There was silence.

"Theodore left as soon as I told him what you said," Ryan continued softly. "He didn't wait until morning."

"Good," Margaret declared. "Laurel should know. I'd come there in a minute if I could, Ryan, but I haven't any way to get there."

"It's okay," Ryan said, sighing. "Your uncle is

going to take me home in a little while. He says I need to get my rest and something to eat."

A recording came on the phone. "Please deposit thirty cents for the next ten minutes."

"I haven't got thirty cents, Margaret," Ryan shouted. "There's something wrong with this phone. This is a local call. Anyway, one more thing. You know that kid, Darcy?"

"Yeah?" Margaret yelled back. "Darcy Lupus?"

"Thirty cents please," the recording moaned at them. "Please deposit thirty cents for the next three minutes."

"Yeah, her. Well I saw her in the park. She was with a swan, and I couldn't really see the swan from the back but it looked like . . ."

The line went dead and only the dial tone buzzed in Margaret's ear.

5

DARCY'S SECRET

Somehow Margaret made it through breakfast that morning. She didn't really feel like eating, but she forced herself because she thought she should. She was sleep deprived and needed the energy. She hadn't been able to go back to sleep since Ryan's call. Instead she had spent the early hours pacing the living room floor. She had tried to call him about 6:30 but there was no answer. His truncated phone call left her confused and bewildered. What could he possibly have wanted to tell her about Darcy? She was just finishing her last sip of orange juice when the phone rang again.

Margaret rushed to answer it, hoping it was Ryan. She was dying to know what he had started to tell her before the pay phone cut him off and she had to practically sit on her hands to keep from dialing his number every five minutes. Ryan had been through enough last night and needed his sleep, she told herself, even if he was home by now.

She had to try to control her curiosity. The phone call wasn't Ryan anyway, it was Uncle John.

"How are you, Margaret?" his weary voice trailed over the phone.

"Fine," Margaret replied crisply. "How's Wilda?"

"Holding her own, that's the best I can say. I'll be home in a while to get some rest. I'm bushed."

"Will she live?" Margaret asked, wishing her uncle would be more specific.

"That remains to be seen," Uncle John told her. "She's fighting for every breath she takes. If there's a way to come out of this, I have confidence that she'll find it."

Margaret clicked down the receiver and flopped on the couch. Maybe she should call Ryan again. He probably needed a friend now anyway. Perhaps Theodore had returned and had some news from Laurel. Even though she had just seen him last night, Margaret longed for some word from the swan. Advice. Encouragement. Anything to help her know how to fight off Sebastian's dreadful attack.

She didn't know what to do to help Wilda. She felt as if Laurel had expected her to do something to thwart Sebastian's plan, but she was at a loss to know what it was. She remembered what Laurel had told her about the invisible rainbows that arched over Sebastian's places of devastation. She imagined a brilliant one arching over Wilda's bed, sending light rays of health into her body. It made her feel better.

She was on her way to the phone when there

was a loud rapping at the door. That was odd. Most people rang the doorbell when they came to the house. Margaret winked one eye shut and peered suspiciously out the peephole. There stood pale Darcy Lupus, her mouse-brown hair blowing wildly in the blustery wind. Her eyes were sunken and her skin appeared more moley than usual. Margaret flung the door open and Darcy came into the living room breathing heavily.

"Oh Margaret," she gasped. "I've just got to talk with you. Where on earth were you last night?"

"Nowhere on earth," Margaret stated bluntly. "Come and sit down."

"I don't have long," Darcy told her, sprawling across the couch. "I've got dance class down at the Old Barn at ten. If mother knew I was here, she'd kill me."

The Old Barn was a kind of community center in town, and even though it was old and splintery, it's huge floor and high ceilings made it a great place for all kinds of events from dancing to volleyball to rummage sales. Margaret loved the Old Barn with its smell of aged wood and sawdust.

"Why?" asked Margaret, surveying Darcy curiously. "You're not doing anything wrong."

"I know," Darcy confessed, "but Mom likes me to get there early to do my warm-up exercises. She usually drives me, but I convinced her to let me walk this time. I hate ballet. I wouldn't do it at all except that mother makes me. Look at this ridiculous purple leotard!"

Darcy opened up her beige spring jacket to reveal a lavender leotard complete with a netted tutu and pink tights.

"I look so stupid!" Darcy moaned.

Margaret giggled in spite of herself.

"It is rather different."

"Anyway," Darcy continued, "I've just got to talk with you."

Something in the way Darcy said it sent a chill down Margaret's spine. She sat in the wicker rocker across from Darcy who sat, stiff and rod-like on the very edge of the couch, her pink knees together and her flat little white sneakers pointing straight ahead.

"Oh, Margaret," Darcy began in hushed tones. "Margaret, there's a swan around here. You won't believe this, but Margaret, he's been talking with me."

Margaret just sat and stared at Darcy. She couldn't believe her ears. "Yes, it's true, Margaret," Darcy said, nodding her head up and down as if it were on a string. "If ever I doubted you before, Margaret, I certainly believe you now. Laurel has appeared to me too. Two times this week."

Margaret finally found her tongue.

"Where . . . where do you meet with him?" she asked.

Her voice was trembling and she could hear it. Suppose Laurel, for whatever reason, had thought it better to meet with Darcy regularly than with her and the others. An odd feeling she was unfamiliar with swept over her. She supposed it was close to jealousy, but it wasn't quite as bold.

"We've met by the weeping willow trees in the park both times," Darcy said in a whisper. "This past Tuesday and Thursday in the afternoon. I saw him first on Tuesday morning on my way to school. I always cut through the park, and on this particular morning this swan was just sitting there right in the middle of my path looking at me. I tried to go around him but he blocked my way. Then he spoke to me, and I was so shocked I dropped all my stuff all over the ground."

"What did he say?" Margaret questioned again, wondering why Laurel had chosen the park instead of the river.

"He said hello in a very polite way and apologized for having made me drop my stuff all over the place. I told him it was quite all right, and that I really had to be going or I'd be late for school. He asked me if I came this way often, and when I said yes he asked if I might meet him after school as he had some important things to tell me. So I said I could and then I left, wondering all the time whether I was dreaming or not. When I went back that afternoon he was waiting for me under the willow tree next to the white bench. You know the one? And I went and sat down next to him and we had a long talk, basically just getting to know each other."

"And that was all?" Margaret asked, feeling terribly left out.

"I met with him again on Thursday," Darcy said,

shrugging. "He's very polite and seems terribly concerned about me."

"So," asked Margaret forcefully, "what did he say?"

"Well, I can't exactly tell you," Darcy said shaking her head. "He made me promise not to tell anyone. He said it was top secret and that only I was chosen to know about it. But Margaret, I feel like if I don't tell someone I will burst. I'm terribly confused about everything he tells me. It's kind of frightening to know so much and keep it all inside. I thought you might be able to help me since you know a lot about swans and magical happenings already."

"I don't think you should tell me if Laurel told you not to," Margaret replied sulkily. "There's usually a reason to the things he asks you not to do."

Darcy looked disappointed.

"Well he shouldn't know I told you," she said softly, "if you don't say anything."

Darcy's eyes pleaded with her and Margaret was perplexed. It was hard to imagine Laurel under the willow tree at the park. She had never seen him there before. It certainly didn't seem fair that Darcy, who had never been to Joona, should be asked to hide secrets from Margaret. Perhaps Darcy was lying. Margaret looked her in the eyes for a few moments. Darcy appeared genuine enough, but her brown eyes had an almost forlorn look to them as if harboring her secrets was not at all a pleasant task.

"All right," conceded Margaret, hoping she was not making a mistake. "But if you tell me I shall have to tell the others."

"You mean the others who went with you to Joona? You can't!" rasped Darcy desperately. "You can't! They're bound to let it slip. Craig probably will be the one. Then I shall be in awful trouble. Besides, the secret involves one of them."

Margaret was getting a bit annoyed. What horrible secret could Darcy be talking about? What awful truth was so important that it had to be kept from the people who were her friends . . . friends who, but for Heather, had shared the secrets of Joona with her since day one.

"Okay," Margaret said with an edge to her voice. "I won't tell anyone. What on earth is the matter, Darcy?"

Darcy wiped her forehead with the back of her hand.

"There's a spy in your group, Margaret," Darcy let out, and then she sighed as if she had just spilled the beans and it had greatly relieved her.

"In our group?" Margaret almost shouted at her. "You mean Craig, Ryan, Heather, and me?"

"Yes," said Darcy and nodded vehemently until Margaret was sure Darcy's head was going to come bobbing off her skinny white neck.

Margaret wasn't sure she wanted to know the dreadful, awful secret now. The whole idea of it seemed to her utterly preposterous and she was becoming rather disturbed. Still, she had promised

Darcy, and her curiosity was getting the better of her. In fact, the note they had received from Theodore warned them of a spy.

"Well?" asked Margaret cautiously. "Who is it?"

"It's Heather," Darcy said so low that Margaret could barely hear. "She's in the service of the dark swan."

"What?" Margaret exclaimed. "What on earth are you saying, Darcy? Heather is one of us now. She couldn't possibly be under Sebastian's influence."

Darcy looked at Margaret long and hard. There was a desperation to her voice as she began talking. Occasionally her voice would break and squeak like a violin.

"She wants you to think she's still on Laurel's side," Darcy launched in. "Laurel told me she had you entirely fooled. He said that even though Heather was on your side and saved your life last time you were in Joona, she has since switched to Sebastian's side and is doing everything she can to cooperate with his devious plans to seek vengeance against you and the others. Sebastian has promised her that she will be princess of Joona instead of you when he destroys you, and she wants that more than anything in the world. Sebastian has promised her all kinds of riches and perfume and a whole case of apricot lip gloss that glows in the dark if she does his bidding. Her task now is to report to him any news she gets about the three of you and your plans to help Laurel."

Margaret's mouth dropped.

"How can this be?" she uttered over and over. "You're lying, Darcy! It can't be true!"

"It's Sebastian's fault," Darcy said bluntly. "He's doing it to her."

"But it doesn't make any sense," Margaret blurted out. "I just saw Laurel only last night. He didn't say anything about any of this to me."

"You saw Laurel?" Darcy queried, her eyes growing wide. "He told me he wasn't going to appear to you right now. Oh well, I guess he changed his mind. Besides, Laurel wouldn't tell you. He felt you would find out about it soon enough, and that when you did, your greatest trial would be what to do about it by Joona law."

"She willingly went over to Sebastian's side," Margaret muttered under her breath, still disbelieving it was true. "That means she belongs to him. That means the lake of sulfur."

"Yes," said Darcy, as if this had all been explained to her at length. "And if you are princess you will be required to sentence her there or go in yourself in her place."

Margaret's head was spinning. The comfort she had felt after seeing Laurel last night was gone. Instead, her heart pounded in her chest and her hands were moist and trembling.

"It's not fair," she said to Darcy. "Laurel should have told me this himself. It's not like him to hide the truth from me."

"I guess I was wrong to tell you, Margaret,"

Darcy admitted, looking down. "But it was too much for me to hold in. I feel better now. I hope you're not too cross with me. I just felt you had to know."

Margaret got up and walked to the window. Then she began to pace back and forth in front of Darcy with her fingers locked together behind her neck. She was sure all of her pacing was going to make a little rut in the floor.

It didn't make sense. The whole thing was so strange. Still, Heather had been known to be an avid double-crosser in her former days. That was, of course, before she had tasted the Joona water and gotten to know Laurel and been changed. Heather was not the same person anymore. Everyone could see that. Still, there was always the possibility that she could have betrayed them if Sebastian had gotten hold of her. Sebastian could be very persuasive.

"When did this happen?" Margaret asked Darcy. "When did Heather go over to the other side?"

Darcy just shrugged.

"Laurel didn't tell me that," she said simply.

Darcy's eyes began to wander about the room. She seemed to not want to talk about it anymore now that she had shared her awful secret. It was Margaret who was now suffering and feeling very much alone.

"I don't know," Margaret kept saying to herself over and over as she shuffled past Darcy again and again. "I just don't know."

"I've got to go," Darcy told Margaret in an absent sort of way.

She got up stiffly from the couch.

"I might be late for dance, you know. The teacher would tell my mother and then I'd get it."

"Okay," said Margaret, annoyed.

Darcy wouldn't be bad if she just had a little more backbone and a mind of her own. She didn't see how Darcy could wear that silly outfit and worry about dance class at a time like this. Still, she held the door open for Darcy and said a polite goodbye. Margaret really didn't want Darcy around now, anyway. She had to think, and to think Margaret needed to be alone.

As she clicked the door shut, the thought that Laurel was excluding her from his meetings with Darcy made her stomach feel all knotted and tense. It was so unlike the swan, and yet perhaps she had done something to offend the great, gentle creature she loved so much. It couldn't be! She had just seen Laurel last night. He was as wonderful to her as he had ever been. There had not been the least hint of disapproval in the swan's mannerisms, but of course there never was.

The phone rang. At first Margaret didn't even hear it, then suddenly she jumped. Running into the kitchen she grabbed the receiver noisily off the hook. This time it was Ryan.

"Hi," he said. "Sorry I didn't call you back sooner, I fell asleep."

"I figured," Margaret retorted, breathless from her sudden dash. "I nearly called you a hundred times. What's going on?"

"Well, I'm off to see my mom. A friend of ours is driving me. They only let you in ten minutes every hour. When I get to be a doctor, I'm changing that stupid rule."

"Is Theodore back?"

"No."

"So what was it you started to say last night about Darcy and Laurel?" Margaret demanded. "I've just got to know. Darcy was here just a few minutes ago. She was acting kind of weird. She gave me a message from Laurel about Heather that I can't talk about. It's confusing me terribly."

"Laurel?" Ryan shot back. "She said she spoke with Laurel?"

"Well, yes," Margaret said. "That's what she said . . ."

"She lied!" Ryan interrupted. "That wasn't Laurel she was talking to in the park. I saw it with my own eyes. That swan was too thin and small. Had that greenish sort of hue to him, too, I'm sure. In fact I heard her! She called him Sebastian. I know she did!"

"Sebastian!" Margaret exclaimed. *Why hadn't she thought of it before?* "Of course!"

She had known Sebastian was here on earth. Laurel had told her. It made perfect sense now. The statement about Heather and the feeling that maybe Laurel didn't like her anymore was all a big lie.

"So Heather's not a spy after all!" Margaret sighed with relief. "Darcy is!"

"Gee whiz, is that what Darcy told you?"

"Why, yes, I suppose it's okay to tell you now. That's exactly what she told me."

"The creep," Ryan said, after a moment's pause. "She wants to divide us. We'll be weaker that way."

"But Ryan, maybe she just needs a little help to sort things through. You know how cunning Sebastian can be."

"Well, maybe," Ryan sighed. "All I know is I wish he'd get out of here. He's really botching things up."

"Theodore will come soon. Then he might have a message for us. I saw Laurel last night, where the swinging bridge used to be. Did you see him too, Ryan?"

"No, I just saw a rainbow. That's why I called you. What did Laurel say?"

"That there is an invisible rainbow arching over every place Sebastian tries to destroy. I am imagining one over your mother's bed, Ryan."

"Gee whiz, thanks," Ryan muttered softly. "I suppose I should get ready to go."

"And I ought to go see if I can help Darcy," Margaret declared. "You know, talk to her a little bit. I have a feeling she has no idea how awful Sebastian really is."

"Sebastian will hate you for it," Ryan warned her. "Be careful."

As soon as they hung up, Margaret scribbled a note to Uncle John on the back of an envelope and left it on the kitchen table. She had the picture of her mother and father inside her overall bib pocket tucked in, along with everything else she always carried from Joona—the star, the magic feather, and the key. If only she had been able to meet her father! She was certain she would have liked him. From the picture he seemed to be just her type. She would have to make a point of getting to know everything she could about him as soon as she got the chance.

Right now, however, she had to get to Darcy. She must stop Sebastian's plans at every juncture if they were to squelch his terrible rage on earth. Things were getting too far out of control. She knew Uncle John still loved Wilda. If Wilda died, Uncle John would never be the same. Ryan and Theodore would be orphaned and probably sent away somewhere. Margaret would never have a real family again. Uncle John might not even want her around anymore. He would send her away to Auntie Emily's dreadful apartment, which would become her home. No, it was up to her, Margaret Morrison, to see that Sebastian did not get the upper hand. She would fight him until she dropped. That was her mission.

She was halfway down the road to the Old Barn when she heard sirens. At first she didn't pay much attention. The sirens were far off in the distance and Margaret figured it was just a couple of police cars stopping some morning speeders. The sound of the sirens kept coming closer and closer until Margaret had to cover her ears. Stopping to look behind her, she saw three fire trucks blazing down the road at rocket speed. They passed her in a whirl of dust and smoke and flashing lights. Margaret watched them go and suddenly her eyes became round with horror. The fire trucks were headed in the same direction she was going. It couldn't be! Yet, with Sebastian on the loose . . . she couldn't think it.

Margaret broke into a wild sprint, not daring to believe it was so. The Old Barn was only a few more blocks toward the center of town and then off to the right. It took her another five minutes to reach it. As it came into view, her heart sank. There were the fire trucks, with men and women in black suits running about. Three of them were holding a big yellow hose spraying water at the wooden building. The barn was engulfed in flames. Others were unloading a second hose from the truck. Thick black smoke poured out of the upstairs windows in heavy billows. Already a small crowd had gathered and police were milling about the scene. Margaret saw an old man standing next to her and pulled desperately at his sleeve.

"What's happening?" she begged. "Tell me what's happening?"

"The old place went up in flames just moments ago," the grizzly old man said shakily. "An electrical fire I 'spect. Mice probably chewed a wire. I heard they were having trouble with a short somewhere and couldn't find the source. Lucky everyone in there got out in time."

The old man had tobacco stains around his mouth.

"Where's the dance class?" Margaret demanded. "Where are the kids who were in the class?"

"Yonder," the old man said, pointing to a cluster of girls on the lawn across the street. "I seen 'em run out together, all in stretch outfits. Just passin' by I was when. . . ."

Margaret didn't wait for the old man to finish. She bolted across the street and quickly scanned the group of girls, some of whom were crying. Others, with wide expressionless faces, stared in shock at the building. The teacher was running about frantically talking to people. To her surprise she saw Heather running toward her.

"Heather, are you okay?" Margaret asked. "Were you in the barn when . . . ?"

Heather nodded and swallowed hard.

"I heard a snapping and then suddenly there was fire up in the loft. I couldn't believe it."

"Is this the class Darcy's in?"

Heather gave a quick nod.

"Then where is she?"

Heather scanned the little cluster of girls.

"She's not here," Heather said, her eyes growing wide. "No wait, I remember. Darcy went into the bathroom for some water just before . . . just before the fire started."

The two girls looked at each other, speechless. Heather's face became white as a ghost. Margaret pressed her lips together so hard they grew numb.

"Margaret!" Heather whispered finally. "She could still be in there!"

"This is Sebastian's doing," Margaret said, her

mouth going dry. "And he is not going to get away with it."

In a flash she bolted back across the street leaving Heather alone on the grass.

"Margaret!" Heather screamed after her. "Margaret, where are you going?"

Margaret didn't answer. There was no time to waste. She thought of trying to speak to one of the firefighters, but she was afraid it would take too long. The roar of the water shooting out from the hoses was deafening and they were all extremely preoccupied. Besides, the whole area was blocked off with a fence of yellow tape so that she could hardly get near them. It would take her forever to get their attention. Then she'd have to explain everything and precious time would be lost. They might not even believe her, and then she'd be worse off than if she'd just done it herself. She found her way around to the back entrance of the barn and ducked under the yellow tape. There was no one around at the moment to send her back. It was extremely hot as she drew near the building, but Margaret knew the Old Barn well. She had come here endless times with her school for special functions. Sometimes they even came to the Old Barn for volleyball since the ceilings were so high. She knew right where the bathrooms were. All she had to do was duck in and check to see if Darcy was there. If not, then she'd simply run out.

The smoke and heat hit her in a suffocating wave as she slipped in the back door. Margaret backed out again and stood for a moment on the step coughing, her eyes burning. She was a fool. The whole building could collapse on her and she'd be dead. Carefully she unzipped her bib pocket and took out her magic feather. Holding it in front of her she closed her eyes tightly. She wasn't sure if the feather worked on earth as well as it did in Joona, but it was worth a try.

"Okay," Margaret whispered. "Let's see now. The poem . . . *'Uprisings of power will shake the kingdom, our lives will be put to the test. For those alone without a friend there will be no rest. Yet in the midst of dark despair, where life is nearly death . . . Laurel who plummets the sulfur sea will awaken in us a victory.'*"

Margaret said it breathlessly and felt a surge of the fountain water bubble inside her. Then she closed her eyes, and with every ounce of courage she could muster she plunged into the Old Barn.

Outside the flames were now lapping around the upstairs windows. Uncle John, who was just getting home from the hospital, pulled his Jeep up on the grass and got out to see if anyone needed medical attention. The crowd, which was now much larger, had been moved back to the opposite side of the street. The same old man Margaret had spoken with was standing near Uncle John as he emerged from his Jeep.

"Lucky everyone got out in time," he wheezed to Uncle John. "It's a pretty bad fire."

"I'll say," said John, looking up at the flames.

A voice came booming out over a loud speaker.

"Attention! Attention please! The building may collapse at any time. Please stand on the opposite side of the street. We repeat: Please cooperate. Stand no closer than the opposite side of the street for your own safety."

Police began waving back a few stubborn spectators.

"Sure looks like it's about ready to fall," Uncle John mused. "It was an old building to begin with. Sort of a landmark."

"We're losing our landmarks in this town," the old man muttered. "First they take down the old swinging bridge, now this goes up in flames."

"John!" a voice screamed. "John Morrison!"

John looked up and saw Heather charging toward him from the other side of the street. Her face was sooty and streaked with tears.

"Heather, what were you doing over there?" Uncle John demanded, taking hold of Heather's arm. "Stay over here! You could get yourself killed."

"No! No! Listen to me," Heather begged.

She pulled out of John's firm hold on her arm and began crying hysterically.

"What is it, Heather?" John asked, stooping down to look her in the eyes. "Calm down, Heather. Tell me now, so I can understand."

Heather was breathing so hard her words came out in short, shallow gasps.

"It's . . . it's Darcy. We think she's still in there." Heather blubbered unabashedly. "And when

85

Margaret found out, she went in after her. I followed her and saw her go in. When I tried to go in, I couldn't. It was too hot and I couldn't breathe."

Uncle John stood up to his full height. His face was completely white.

"She went in the back way," Heather told him. "We thought that's where Darcy might be, 'cause she went to the bathroom for some water just before. . . ."

Uncle John was across the street before Heather finished her sentence.

He jumped the yellow tape and grabbed the shoulder of one of the firefighters.

"Two little girls are in this building," he screamed. "One of them is my niece. Get in there and do something, now!"

6

THE
TRIAL

As soon as Margaret entered the building she was surrounded by a cloud of smoke so thick she couldn't keep her eyes open. Pawing her way forward, she stumbled and fell against the wall. She knew she was only a few feet from the entrance to the girl's restroom. She groped her way forward on hands and knees. The wood against her hands was hot to the touch. Margaret wanted a breath of air so badly she could scarcely keep from bursting. Still, she continued to move forward as quickly as she could, pressing her shoulder against the wall as a guide.

Only a few seconds later her hands came upon something soft. It was the moist flesh of a human being. For a split second Margaret opened her eyes. Through the swirling smoke she could make out that the human form was most certainly Darcy lying face down. She quickly linked her arms around Darcy's arms and began to pull her jerkily toward the door. Margaret was frantic for air and her head was spinning. She felt her strength giving way. She tried to take a breath but only inhaled the fumes from the smoke. She began to cough and gag. Darcy groaned.

It wasn't far now. Just a few more paces. She could make it, she told herself, *if only she didn't give up.* How like Sebastian to deal in fire and smoke! The heat and the smoke reminded her of the heat and the mist from the lake of sulfur in Joona. Margaret suddenly felt a doorknob on her left. All she needed was to push it open and they would be in the fresh air again. Her face and neck were dripping with perspiration. She lost her grip on Darcy momentarily and Darcy fell to the floor like a lead weight. As Margaret reached down to pick her up again, something came crashing down and knocked her in the back. Margaret fell forward and landed next to Darcy with a loud thump; the pain in her back was excruciating. She tried to move, but she was pinned beneath something that was heavy and hot.

Vaguely she heard the announcement for people to remain on the opposite side of the street for their own safety since the building might collapse at any minute. She heard something else come crashing down a little ways off from where she lay. Blinded by the smoke, she reached out desperately for the door, but the fall had knocked her forward and it was now out of reach. Coughing and sputtering for air, she clawed momentarily at the floor with the last little bit of strength she had left. It was futile.

She would die here in the Old Barn and Sebastian would win his wretched victory. Maybe Ryan or Craig or Heather would beat him in the end. She had tried and failed. She put her head down on the hot wooden floor and her thoughts began to tumble over each other like she was being tossed around in a tidal wave. Then everything started to go grayish black. She began coughing heavily now and gagging until she was sure her lungs would burst.

A cool breeze brushed her face and caressed her brow. *Perhaps she was at home now*, Margaret thought deliriously, *and someone had turned on a fan or opened the window*. She took a wild gasp for air and found that it was pure and sweet. What was that aroma? It gave her a sudden burst of hope. The clear air was reviving her and she gulped for more. Straining to open her swollen eyes she suddenly remembered. The aroma was the Joona smell of pine and lilac. She was with Laurel! Perhaps she had died and was now to live with him forever. Maybe now she would be able to fly like a swan and live in the castle with her mother and reign as princess. Her death must have been her greatest trial. Now she was finally free.

Managing to open her eyes a tiny slit, she saw him. He was not standing on the shores of the sparkling Joona waters as she had suspected. Rather, Laurel was standing just inside a burst of glowing flames that shot up behind him like pillars. His wide white wings flapped back and forth faster than Margaret had ever seen them flap. They were creating a draft and moving the smoke away. Laurel kept arching his neck forward and breathing on them through his open beak. Each time he did, the pine and lilac fragrance grew stronger and the air fresher. Margaret could breathe now, deeply and rhythmically. It felt so wonderful to be able to breathe. All around them, flames and smoke sparked and billowed like angry animals ready to come in for the kill. Something else came crashing down behind them, but Margaret closed her eyes and breathed deeply. She might not be in Joona yet, but now that Laurel was here, everything would be okay. Now that Laurel was here, nothing could frighten her.

She felt a draft of a different sort on her legs and realized that someone had opened the outside door.

"They're right here," a voice shouted, and she felt two strong arms grab her forcefully and carry her into the sunlight. "She's still alive."

"This one is too," someone else yelled.

A person had hold of her head now and was breathing into her mouth.

Margaret coughed and sputtered and opened her eyes a tiny slit. She was looking into the face of her uncle. She meant to say something, but her voice wouldn't come out. She closed her eyes again and felt herself drifting in a murky black sea.

"The ambulance is here," a voice announced.

"Please stand back," the loud speaker boomed

out. "The building is caving in. For your own safety, please stand on the opposite side of the street."

Margaret wondered how Darcy was doing but she couldn't make herself wake up. The black sea was too relaxing. She let herself go to it and everything else faded away.

❮❮❮

Something was beeping a loud persistent beep that sounded at regular intervals. Maybe it was the alarm clock. If Margaret were late for school again she would get detention. Her alarm clock sounded different, though. It had a long continuous ring rather than a succession of beeps. Perhaps Uncle John had set the timer for his famous meat loaf and the timer was going off again and again because there was no one to turn it off. If no one turned it off or took the meat loaf out of the oven, the meat loaf would burn. The oven would get so hot that the whole house might go up in flames. The smoke would suffocate her and swallow her alive. She'd be gasping for breath, struggling in the heavy smoke to find her way out of the house, but it would be no use. Margaret had to get up and turn that timer off.

She felt a sharp stab of pain in her back as she tried to move. She opened her eyes and saw a nurse with short red hair fiddling with a plastic tube that came out of a bottle. The bottle hung upside-down on a pole by Margaret's head. The nurse looked down at Margaret and smiled.

"So you decided to finally wake up, did you?" she remarked kindly. "Do you remember your name?"

Margaret nodded.

"Margaret," she whispered through dry lips that would hardly move.

"Good," said the nurse pleasantly. "I see you've got your wits about you. You're in the hospital and we're just giving you a little bit of fluid through this tube is all. When the bottle goes dry the buzzer beeps. Don't worry about it. Seems to me like you must have a guardian angel or someone looking after you anyway. You hardly needed any oxygen, and you got pulled from that building just seconds before the whole thing collapsed."

Margaret looked up at the nurse too tired to say anything. The whole experience in the Old Barn suddenly came flooding back to her. She desperately wanted to find out how Darcy was, but she couldn't form the words right. The nurse answered her question in the next breath.

"Seems like the little friend you went to rescue is doing fine. She went home with her parents a while ago after everything checked out normal. Her whole family came in here to see you before they left and your uncle has been watching you carefully all day. He went down to get something to eat at the snack bar just a few moments before you woke up. He'll be back. Now, see this little button on the wall? If you need anything, anything at all, you be sure to push it and one of us on duty will come."

"Can I go home, too?" Margaret finally managed to rasp, loud enough for the nurse to hear.

The nurse paused.

"Of course you'll be able to go home, eventually," she finally said hesitantly. "Right now though, you're here to rest, and rest you shall. Sometimes resting up takes time, so don't be impatient. Now relax. Do you feel like eating?"

Margaret shook her head.

The nurse left the door ajar and slipped out into the hall. Margaret didn't understand why Darcy got to go home and she had to stay. Maybe it was because Uncle John was a doctor and he had requested it. She looked out the window and the sky was dark. She had no idea what time it was. Her legs felt numb and her throat was sore. The plastic tube had been inserted into her right arm with a needle and there was white tape holding it in place. It didn't hurt, it was just awkward when she turned from side to side. She really couldn't turn though; her back hurt too much. She looked over at the little table by her bed. There was the photograph of her mother and dad that had been in her overall bib pocket propped against the lamp. Uncle John must have put it there for her to see when she woke up. She looked down and saw that she was wearing a white cotton hospital gown. Margaret missed her overalls and began to worry if her star, magic feather, and key to Joona were safe.

Just then someone pushed the door open wide. Uncle John came striding into the room with a

Styrofoam cup of coffee in his hand. He had on his hospital coat and his name tag. Margaret thought he definitely looked like a doctor.

"Well, hello there," he said, grinning at her. "Do you remember me?"

Margaret nodded and smiled a tiny smile.

"Good!" John said happily, going over to her bedside. "The nurse paged me and told me you were awake. How do you feel?"

He planted a kiss on her forehead.

"I'm okay," Margaret told him softly. "Help me sit up."

"Not yet, honey," her uncle said, gently brushing back the hair from her face. "It's important that you just lie flat right now and rest. You've been unconscious for the last four hours, so just take it real easy."

"When can I go home?" Margaret asked him, hoping he would smile again and tell her she could go home this very minute if she promised to be good.

"Well, I'm not sure," John said slowly. "You were very brave to go in after Darcy, Margaret. You saved her life, you know."

"I didn't get her out," Margaret said regretfully. "I tried, but this thing fell on me and I couldn't move. The nurse said she went home and she's fine now, right?"

Uncle John did smile then. He took her hand in his and sat down on the edge of the bed.

"You are unbelievable, Margaret," he said, shaking his head in disbelief. "I don't know what to make of you. On one hand, going into a burning building is insane. I know you know that, and the fact that you did it without getting help first upsets me. On the other hand, if you hadn't gone in there right away and brought Darcy to the door, we'd have never found her. There wasn't time. The building collapsed just moments after we got the two of you out. I'm amazed at your courage. Very few people would have been able to do what you did. You sacrificed everything. I am just beginning to realize that I almost lost you."

Uncle John's eyes were filling with tears and he quickly blinked them back. Margaret smiled weakly.

"I had the words from the poem," Margaret told him. "It helped a lot."

Uncle John didn't seem to understand what Margaret was talking about and just patted her hand over and over. Margaret was too weak to explain. Her uncle seemed to want to tell her something that he couldn't quite bring himself to say.

"How's your back feel, Margaret?" he asked her finally, very softly.

"It hurts me when I try to move."

There was a lengthy pause.

"Your legs? How do they feel?"

"Sort of numb, like they've fallen asleep."

"Well," John said finally, his voice getting caught in his throat. "Is there anything I can get you? Anything you'd like to have?"

"Are my feather, star, and key safe?"

Uncle John nodded.

"I put them in your jewelry box at home. I didn't think they'd be safe here. I did keep the picture of your mom and dad here for you though."

"Thanks," said Margaret. "Can I put my overalls back on?"

There was another lengthy pause.

"What's wrong?" Margaret asked him.

She knew Uncle John too well. He wasn't telling her something.

"It's not Wilda, is it?" Margaret demanded suddenly. "She didn't die, did she?"

Uncle John chuckled. It felt good to hear him chuckle.

"Oh, Margaret," he began, a light coming back into his eyes. "Wilda took a sudden turn for the better just a few hours ago. They moved her out of ICU and she's on the general ward now. I spoke to her a little while ago. She wants to come and see you just as soon as she's strong enough. It looks like I'm going to be at the hospital night and day with the two people I love the most in the whole world here together."

"Yea!" Margaret cheered as loud as she was able. "I knew Sebastian wouldn't triumph. I knew it wouldn't work out the way he planned."

"And to add to that," Uncle John continued. "You might be interested to know that Wilda and I will be married next May."

"You actually came right out and asked her?"

Margaret said hoarsely, the smile growing on her face. "I never thought you'd do it without asking me what to say first."

John gave Margaret a light playful punch on her shoulder.

"That'll be enough smart alecky stuff," he teased. "Who made you such an expert on people's romantic lives anyway?"

Margaret shrugged and looked at her uncle to see if his appearance had changed at all since he had decided to get married. She didn't really see any major differences. She knew that sometimes after people got married they became chubby, but Uncle John was so tall and lean she doubted that would happen. He didn't seem to be gaining any weight so far. Perhaps, thought Margaret, he looked a little bit more relaxed in his face, and that made him look more like a family man than a bachelor.

As to Wilda, Ryan, and Theodore making up what would be her family, Margaret had no protest. Wilda believed in Laurel, and she was someone Margaret thought would make an excellent second mother. Ryan had told her once that Wilda never yelled, and Margaret liked that. She liked the flowers that Wilda loved to grow around the house. She also liked that Wilda helped out all the sick animals Theodore found and brought home to their shed. Sometimes Wilda seemed more like a kid than a grownup because she was so easy to talk to. Wilda laughed easily too. As for Ryan and Theodore, they seemed like they were her brothers already.

Nothing could bring them closer than they already were. It seemed fitting that they should live under the same roof as a family since all of them shared the same love for Laurel and Joona.

"There's someone here to see you," Uncle John said suddenly, getting to his feet.

Margaret looked up. She saw Darcy with a big bandage across her forehead stride toward her. When Darcy reached Margaret she bent down and gave her a gigantic hug. Margaret waited for Darcy to stop hugging her and stand up again, but she didn't for a long time. Instead she felt Darcy's body heaving up and down on her chest. She patted Darcy on the back and told her everything was okay now.

"Margaret," Darcy said, finally standing up again, her cheeks stained with tears. "You saved my life, Margaret. I am the worst person you could have saved, Margaret. The very worst of the worst."

"Stop it, Darcy!" Margaret demanded. "I did it because you're my friend. What other reason did I need?"

"Margaret," said a woman's voice.

It was Mary Lupus. She still had those skinny blue eyes, but they weren't nearly as piercing as Margaret remembered them. She was standing at the foot of Margaret's bed and smiling a broad smile.

"I think we'll leave the two of you alone for a little while to talk," she began warmly. "It seems as though you two have some things to discuss. I just want to thank you, Margaret, for saving my daughter's life. There is no way to repay you for what you did. You are a very courageous young lady."

"Thank you," Margaret replied softly.

Mary Lupus and Uncle John left the room, clicking the door shut behind them. Margaret looked at Darcy apprehensively. What side was she on now anyway? She waited for Darcy to speak. If Margaret spoke first she was afraid she might give crucial secrets away to the wrong person.

"Margaret," Darcy said in the smallest form of a whisper, putting her head down and picking at her nails. "I knew."

"What on earth are you talking about?"

"I lied to you, Margaret." Darcy's voice was shaking. "I am so ashamed of myself. You are so good, and I am so, so awful. You should have let me burn, Margaret. It's where I belong. In the fires of hell."

"You sound like you've gone nuts," Margaret retorted. "Completely nuts."

Darcy took a deep breath.

"I knew, Margaret," she said again. "I knew it was Sebastian and not Laurel I was talking to in the park. We met many more times than I told you—at least sixteen times. Sebastian told me to convince my mother to tear down the old bridge. Then after that he told me to tell you he was Laurel. He told me to try to make you jealous and that if I got your group split up and mad at each other he would reward me. He promised me all these things, Margaret. Like straight A's next semester and fruit candies under my pillow every night. He said I would reign as queen in Joona if I would be his spy, and that anything I wanted would be mine. He would talk with me, and his eyes had this steady glaze to them that hypnotized me. It was like I was in a trance, although if I had really wanted to back out of it, I suppose I could have. It just sounded so wonderful that I hardly thought about what it all meant. At night I dreamed about being queen and sleeping on satin pillows and cushy down comforters. During the day, all I could think about was having more fruit candies. He gave me one each time we met, but I was never satisfied. All I wanted was more. It was like I was always living for some future promise he kept telling me would be mine if only I would just do one more thing for him. I guess I was sort of jealous of you to begin with. I wished I was part of your group, sailing off to Joona. I thought at least this way I might get involved. Through the back door, so to speak."

Margaret gazed into Darcy's thin, pale face and wondered what to say next. She wasn't angry. She wasn't surprised either. Her main thought was what a jerk Sebastian was.

There was a lengthy pause in which Darcy, still picking at her nails, said hoarsely, "I understand if you never want to talk with me again, Margaret. If you want me to leave right this minute, just tell me and I'll go."

The red-haired nurse opened the door and stood for a moment in the door frame.

"How are you, miss?" she asked pleasantly.

Margaret nodded. "Okay."

"They'll be coming down in a few minutes to take you off to X-ray. Your uncle's waiting outside to go with you."

"Okay," Margaret said again.

The nurse left and closed the door. Margaret wondered why she had to go to X-ray now. She just wanted to go home.

"I guess I should be on my way," Darcy mumbled. "Probably the very sight of me is revolting to you."

"Cut it out," Margaret heard herself say. "You were my friend. You still are my friend as long as . . . as long as. . . ."

"What?" Darcy asked.

"As long as I can know that it's safe to trust you again."

Darcy flinched. "You mean I could be lying right now, right?"

Margaret shrugged. "Yes, I guess that's what I mean."

"Margaret," Darcy said earnestly. "Would it make a difference if I told you I saw the real Laurel? Because I did. When I saw him I knew right away who he was. He was standing in the flames in that building, Margaret. He was breathing on us and flapping the smoke away from us with his great white wings so we could breathe. I've never seen such a big, glorious swan before. I don't know how I knew it, but when I saw him I had this sense deep inside myself that he forgave me. And when I looked into his eyes I realized that it was Laurel I wanted to follow, not Sebastian. Laurel is who I'd wanted all along—I just hadn't realized how ugly Sebastian was until I saw Laurel. Do you believe me, Margaret? How could you possibly believe me . . . ?"

Darcy's voice trailed away, and she looked at Margaret, despair written across her face.

"I do believe you," Margaret said. "I believe you completely."

"Why?" Darcy asked. "Why on earth would you?"

Margaret took Darcy's hand and squeezed it.

"I saw him too," Margaret told her. "Just as you described."

"Can I be on your side then?" Darcy asked, pleadingly. "From now on? I want to be, if you'll only let me."

"Of course," Margaret assured her. "Laurel wants you, and so do I."

The door opened again, and this time Uncle John and Mary Lupus were standing there.

"The X-ray people are here," Mary Lupus announced. "Come along, Darcy. We'll visit Margaret again."

"Okay," said Darcy reluctantly. "Thanks, Margaret, for everything."

She made her way toward the door.

"I forgot to ask," Margaret called after her. "Is your forehead hurt badly?"

Darcy shook her head. "Just burned it a little.

Sort of hurts, but nothing serious. I've got to put this disgusting ointment stuff on it twice a day."

Mary Lupus and Darcy left, and as they did, two men in white rolled a bed on wheels into the room.

"Excuse me," Uncle John said, elbowing his way past them into the room. "I need a few moments with my niece. Please wait outside. There's something I must tell her."

"Dr. Morrison," one of them said, "X-ray is overbooked today and we're running on a tight schedule. We really must. . . ."

"I need a few minutes," Uncle John interrupted, quite sternly. "Leave us alone, please."

"Can I go home after I go to X-ray?" Margaret begged Uncle John when the disgruntled X-ray people had left. "I'll rest, I promise! Hospitals give me the creeps. I can't believe you went to school all those years just so you could work in one. Seems like an awful place to come every single day of your life, especially when you're not sick."

Uncle John smiled briefly and pushed Margaret's hair away from her face like he always did.

"Do you know why you're going to X-ray, Margaret?" he asked soberly.

"I don't have any idea," Margaret piped back at him. "And I think it's very unfair that Darcy gets to go home before I do."

"It's your back, Margaret," her uncle said haltingly.

Margaret could see that it was difficult for Uncle

John to talk. Every so often he would cough in the middle of his sentence, but Margaret thought what he really wanted to do was cry.

"It appears right now that you have a serious back injury," John continued. "A heavy beam fell across your back when you were in the barn. They did a series of X-rays earlier. One of your vertebrae in your cervical region—I mean your lower back— was damaged. They are taking another set of X-rays now to make sure the first ones were accurate. There is definite nerve damage. That's why you feel numbness and tingling in your legs. You will have to have surgery as soon as possible, so that no further damage results. I've got the best surgeon I know working on this for me."

"After I have surgery, then can I go home?" Margaret persisted hopefully.

Uncle John sighed. "Eventually."

Margaret knew he still wasn't telling her something. Uncle John looked down at his niece with a helpless expression.

"I'm going to see that you get the very best of care while you're here, but I'm not going to lie to you, Margaret. The fact of the matter is that you have a very serious injury. It will be a virtual miracle if you ever walk again."

7

LAUREL RESPONDS

Theodore stood at the edge of a grassy cliff, his arms outstretched to the sky, his face looking upward. Below him, a craggy gorge slit downward at sharp ominous angles while the mountains looming up around him shut out the late afternoon haze. It was drizzling slightly but still Theodore searched the sky, scanning back and forth as if he were reading words etched across the cloudy heavens. He stood there large and motionless like a man preparing for a cleanly executed dive off the edge of a precipice. Any ordinary person would have grown weary holding their arms above their head for so long, but Theodore was strong and unflinching. He seemed almost to be in a posture that was beckoning someone. A posture intended to call someone forth.

Finally he saw what he was looking for and his somber face broke into a wide open grin. Far above him, the slim silhouette of a bird could be seen, circling slowly. With each circle it descended lower and lower in the sky. Theodore didn't move. Laurel descended and enfolded the giant of a boy in his great white wings. Not a sound passed between them. They began to walk silently about the grassy area, heads bent low as if communicating something of extreme importance that was too vital for words. Finally Laurel spoke quietly to Theodore as if referring to something one of them had just said, although to the common ear only silence had passed between them.

"It's her father," Laurel was saying. "He must be restored to her. She knows who he is now and it is vital that we find him to complete all things."

Theodore bent down and picked up a seeded dandelion. He blew the tiny wisps and they were caught by the air and taken up and over the precipice to the gorge below. Then he turned and smiled at Laurel.

"Yes, Theodore," Laurel agreed. "To every time there is a season. It is time to search the shadowy regions for Grant. I alone can do that, for Milohe has given only me the keys to release the dead. Margaret's willing sacrifice for Darcy has vanquished any hold Sebastian had on Grant. He is free now, yet he continues to wander because he cannot find his way. I will bring him and any captives who wish to follow. I shall leave tonight and will be back before dawn to take Margaret with me. You must bring the rest from earth to attend the Great Festal Gathering."

Theodore nodded and cocked his enormous head to one side. His face was puckered in a frown.

"Ah, Theodore! Not to worry!" Laurel crooned. "Your mother is doing fine. Margaret's sacrifice saw to it. Sebastian's power has been deactivated."

With that, the great swan took off but not upward. Rather, he descended rapidly into the craggy gorge that pierced the surface of the earth like jagged knives miles long. Theodore got down on his knees and watched the swan grow smaller and smaller as he disappeared into the earth's open cavern. Finally the swan was swallowed up by the shadows and Theodore could see him no more.

←←←

When Margaret woke up, it was night. The red-haired nurse had made her take a little pill and it had completely wiped her out. Her room was dark, and all she could see was a lone street light that shone in her window like a tiny yellow moon. She looked at the digital clock by her bed—4:45 a.m. She flicked on the table lamp and saw a note propped up in front of the picture of her parents. It was from Uncle John.

Margaret—I went to get some sleep in the doctor's quarters on the third floor. You can page me if you need me by dialing 0452 on the telephone. Your surgery is scheduled for tomorrow morning, at 7:30 a.m. I will be in at 6:30 a.m. to get you ready. Ryan, Heather, and Craig came by to see you earlier, but we couldn't rouse you. Love you so. Uncle John.

So they were going to do surgery! That was the

last thing Margaret wanted. She propped herself up on her elbow. She had no pain right now, and she was convinced that if she could only swing her legs over the side of her miserable, hot little bed, she would be able to walk right out of her horrid hospital room and into the fresh night air. Hospitals were much too white for Margaret and far too quiet. Plus, her room smelled of strange soaps and alcohol, and it was making her feel sick.

Gradually she pulled herself into a sitting position. Then she attempted to get her legs to move themselves. Try as she could, they wouldn't budge. They were like lead weights at the end of her body. She pulled the covers away and stared at them. They stuck out from her flimsy hospital gown like long, white sticks. They didn't seem to belong to her, although she recognized them.

There was the scar on the top of her right knee that she had gotten when she fell off her bike at age six and needed twelve stitches. There was the tiny freckle on her left thigh and the black toenail on her large left toe, which she had gotten caught in the screen door a week ago. Yes, those were her legs. They were attached to her but they weren't doing anything to prove it.

She lifted first one and then the other toward the edge of the bed. It seemed like forever, but finally she sat with both of them dangling down over the side, preparing to launch forward. She was just about to give it a try when a white nurse came in with a thermometer in her hand.

"Miss Morrison!" the nurse cried out.

She was not the red-haired nurse. This nurse had black hair that turned out at the bottom and bangs that hung into her eyes. "Get yourself back into bed this instant!"

"I want to see if I can walk," Margaret protested. "I think I can."

"Miss Morrison!" the nurse exclaimed again, bustling over to her. "You have extensive damage to your lower spine and there is no way you could possibly even stand let alone walk. Now you cooperate like a good girl. You could damage yourself even more if you act foolishly."

"But it doesn't hurt," Margaret argued.

"It doesn't hurt because you're on a painkiller just now. Come on! Up with those legs and back to bed. You're scheduled for surgery tomorrow and you need your rest."

The nurse half-lifted, half-pushed Margaret back into her bed.

Margaret began to cry quietly. She had never felt so frustrated.

"Let me get you something to help you sleep," the nurse offered, and she left a little dixie cup of water and a red pill on Margaret's bedside table.

Then she flicked off the light and was gone. Margaret drank the water but didn't take the pill. She didn't want to sleep. She wasn't tired. She wanted to think. If only she had her magic feather!

"Laurel!" she whispered in the stillness of the dark room. "Laurel, I don't have my magic feather, but I was wondering if perhaps, just maybe, you might come and help me anyway. If this is my trial, Laurel, then I think I shall die without you."

Nothing happened. Margaret hadn't really expected anything to happen anyway. Obviously Laurel couldn't hear her without the magic feather.

She turned her back to the window and lay on her side. She was bored beyond compare. How could Uncle John bear to work in this place day after day? She would much rather be a forest ranger when she grew up or a lifeguard. Even a gardener or a farmer would be better than being cooped up all day in a dull, quiet place like this—with a bunch of people walking around with serious expressions on their faces, giving out shots. Ryan had his heart set on being a doctor as well, and Margaret couldn't understand it. Margaret would do anything to be outside rather than inside. Of course, she certainly couldn't think about being any of the things she wanted to be if she couldn't even walk. Life was over and she was only twelve years old.

A light tapping on the window made Margaret turn quickly around. She blinked several times and then propped herself up on her elbow to make sure she was seeing clearly. It was no mirage. Standing in the glow of the street light was a large white swan perched precariously on the skinny brick window ledge outside. The yellow street light made a halo all around him. He had his head cocked to one side and his neck was bent down low. Laurel was smiling.

8

ESCAPE
TO JOONA

Laurel tapped on the window several times and seemed to be waiting for Margaret to get up and open it. Margaret tried to signal to Laurel that she was bedridden.

"I can't walk!" she finally yelled, but she was convinced that Laurel couldn't hear her through the thick-paned hospital glass.

She struggled to sit up again. Laurel was looking at her with concern and kept cocking his head from one side to the other. Then suddenly, he took off to the night sky. Margaret's heart sank. She wondered if he was coming back sooner than later. She needed help now. Quickly she pushed the button by her bed.

The nurse with the long bangs reappeared in the door.

"My goodness!" she said. "I thought for sure you'd be asleep by now!"

"Would you mind opening the window for me?"

Margaret asked her politely. "It's awfully stuffy in here."

"The A/C is on," the nurse objected. "It's pleasant in here."

"Please," begged Margaret. "I want some fresh air. This room smell funny."

"Very well," the nurse obliged. "Although we're not really supposed to."

The nurse went over to the window and flipped open the lock. Then she struggled with it for a few moments. The window seemed to be stuck shut in the worst way, perhaps because it had been closed for so long. It was the kind of window that was supposed to open sideways. Finally the nurse managed to yank it open a few inches. Just wide enough, thought Margaret, for Laurel to squeeze through.

"That's as best as I can do," the nurse said wearily. "It won't budge any further."

"Thank you," said Margaret.

The nurse left. Margaret relaxed and lay back waiting for Laurel. She watched the sky outside her window turn from blue-black to morning gray. The birds began to chirp and traffic sounds began to pick up on the street below. Still she waited. The big clock on the wall said 6:17. She didn't like that clock. It looked too much like her clock at school, big and round with bold black numbers staring at her. The clock's second hand didn't travel around the face of the clock smoothly and evenly either. It got from number to number by making tiny little jerks. As the sky got lighter, the jerky little second hand made Margaret more and more nervous.

Uncle John was coming in less than half an hour to see her. If Laurel waited too much longer to return, Margaret would have to go to surgery and then be destined to spend months recuperating after which she still wouldn't be able to walk. It didn't make sense.

A hot stab of pain in her back brought tears to Margaret's eyes. Her painkiller must be wearing off. As they had been all morning, her eyes searched the sky for Laurel. Suddenly she became aware that someone else was in the room with her. Turning her head she saw Theodore standing next to her bed. He was holding onto the bed railing with his big meaty hands and his eyes were smiling at her. His mouth was too, turned upward in a crooked grin. On his head he wore a huge straw hat and his clothes smelled of freshly mown grass and earth.

"Theodore!" Margaret exclaimed. "How did you get in here? They won't let visitors in until the afternoon."

Theodore just shrugged. He reached into his pocket and drew out a slightly disheveled bouquet of lilacs and handed them to her.

"Thank you, Theodore," Margaret said, holding the flowers to her nose. "Oh Theodore! I am so glad to see you. You see, Laurel was here in the middle of the night. . . ."

She stopped. Something was rustling at the window. Margaret felt a surge of hope seize her as she turned her head around. Laurel was perched on the wide window pane inside the room, his neck bent down low in a swan smile.

"Greetings!" the swan declared with compassion brimming in his eyes. "Oh Margaret—how glad I am to see you. I have been thinking about you constantly and couldn't wait to come and take you away from here. It must be so dull for you, stuck in this room. I am amazed that landbred creatures are able to recover and heal in such sterile surroundings. I think I might need a few plants, maybe a small fountain, and perhaps a few great paintings to gaze upon. . . . No matter. I my feathered opinion you've been bedridden long enough. It is high time you were swanridden."

"Oh Laurel!" was all Margaret could say.

Before she knew what was happening, Laurel flew into the room, circled once around and landed on her bed. Margaret wrapped her arms around the swan's slender neck and hugged him to her.

"Yes Laurel! Take me away, Laurel! Take me away from this wretched place."

"Only too glad to oblige," the swan whispered in her ear. "And a good job you've done. You have been brave, Margaret. Extremely brave and faithful to the core. Get up on my back now, and we shall soar!"

"I can't move very easily," Margaret told the swan glumly. "My legs won't work."

"Yes," the swan retorted as if it were only a small matter, "I know. I have been following your condition closely. Not to worry. I brought Theodore along for the purpose of expressing you out of here. Theodore!"

Immediately Margaret felt Theodore's arms around her, lifting her up with such ease and gentleness. He placed her carefully on Laurel's back. Margaret noticed she had a little pain but that it didn't seem to matter now. She was with Laurel. Leaning forward she grabbed onto the base of Laurel's neck and let her legs stretch out behind her. She was more comfortable that way.

"And now," said Laurel to Theodore. "You know what to do next? You know how to summon the others?"

Theodore nodded. The swan spread out his wide white wings and rose off the bed as smoothly and quietly as a helium balloon caught by the breeze. Then they coasted gracefully out the window. A moment later Uncle John came in the room to check on Margaret. He hadn't been able to sleep all night. He had been worried about Margaret and the impending surgery. When he saw the big white swan through the open window sailing away with his niece astride, his face fell. Theodore looked at him and smiled as if what was taking place was the most natural thing in all the world.

Uncle John ran to the open window. Margaret and Laurel were already a fair distance away, headed for the distant hills.

"Margaret!" he called. "Come back! Any movement may further damage your back. You must be very careful! Come back!"

Margaret heard her uncle calling from what seemed to be far away. She reached out her arm and waved to him.

"Goodbye, Uncle John!" she shouted as loudly as she could. "I am with Laurel. Nothing can hurt me now!"

Margaret was glad she was far enough away from Uncle John so that she didn't have to stop and explain. She felt bad about leaving so abruptly but she couldn't bear the thought of staying in that hospital room one moment longer. Even if she never walked again, flying on Laurel's back could take the place of walking any day as far as she was concerned. Perhaps his wings could be her legs.

"Are we going to Joona, Laurel?" she asked the swan, as the smell of coffee and donuts from a nearby bakery blew up into her face.

"Yes," said Laurel excitedly. "And not only that, Margaret. I am taking you to see Milohe himself. He is waiting to receive you."

"You are?" asked Margaret astounded. "How can that be? You told me that if I were to walk through the archway at the end of the rainbow where Milohe lives, I would die."

"That was before you laid down your life to save someone else," Laurel told her. His voice was rich with heartfelt gratitude. "Not only did you lay it down, but you laid it down willingly for someone who was Sebastian's accessory. It has never been done before by a landbred creature in the history of Joona. Landbred creatures have fought the enemy and squelched them, but only for a limited period of time. You fought, but you fought differently. By being willing to sacrifice everything you have won everything, Margaret. Sebastian is defeated."

"How come?" asked Margaret, as Laurel bounced lightly over a few wayward currents.

"It is rather complicated, actually," the swan said with a sigh. "Once you get to know how all the magic works, and the principles on which Joona was founded, you might get rather confused. I suppose volumes could be written about it."

Laurel banked to the right. They were flying low over the tops of trees now and the hills were just ahead.

"It actually all boils down to the simple fact that you were able to love far more than Sebastian was able to hate. He goes as far as he can, and you go farther still. It leaves him with nowhere to turn. It leaves him powerless."

"I only did what I thought you would do, Laurel," Margaret confessed. "It didn't seem so terribly sacrificial at the time."

"Sebastian shall stand trial before you, Margaret," Laurel told her soberly. "You shall be his judge."

Margaret grabbed the swan's neck a bit more firmly and pulled herself forward. She wasn't sure she had heard right. The breeze was gusting now and the blue hills rose up on either side of them like the humps of large camels.

"What did you say?" Margaret asked the swan, hoping she had heard incorrectly.

"Sebastian shall stand trial before you, Margaret," Laurel repeated. "You shall be his judge."

"That's what I thought you said!" Margaret blurted out. "I'm no judge, Laurel. That's the last thing I want to do!"

"You have been cruelly injured by his dark magic," Laurel explained firmly. "He knocked your feet out from under you and assumed you wouldn't have a leg to stand on. He underestimated your loyalty and fervor, of course, being the regular bird brain that he is (and I mean that of course in the lowest sense of the term). By Joona law, your verdict is his fate."

"I don't want to," Margaret insisted. "That is too horrible."

"If you do not judge him, then Milohe will simply destroy him," Laurel said with grave seriousness. "By not judging him, you have pronounced him dead."

"You mean if I don't, that's it?" Margaret asked astounded. "And what about Darcy? She knowingly went over to Sebastian's side. Doesn't that mean the lake of sulfur for her unless I go in her place?"

"You already gave your life willingly to save hers," Laurel said, again with great gratitude. "That contract is settled. Sebastian is our only liability now. You are the one who holds Sebastian's destiny, Margaret."

They were descending to the clearing next to the cave. As they got lower in the sky, Margaret gasped.

"Laurel! My key! My star! The feather! They were taken from me in the hospital. I forgot all about it until this minute."

"It is okay, Margaret," Laurel assured her. "You shall now enter Joona the way I do, and the way Theodore does. There is another entrance that does not require a key. As for right of passage, our journey is to Milohe this time. We do not need to land until then."

They flew past the door in the rock flying very close to the top of the trees. Many of the pine trees were a mixture of dark green at the center and lighter green out toward the branches. Margaret could see it clearly from the sky and thought the forest definitely looked enchanted. As they swept over a small hill Margaret jumped. A rainbow arched over a cavelike opening in the ground. A bubbling fountain springing up from the rocky soil gushed down into it. The fountain was immense. It picked up the light from the rainbow and played with it in a glistening, swirling harmony of color.

"Here we are, Margaret," Laurel said. "The beginning of the waterfall. Our entrance."

"The rainbow!" Margaret exclaimed. "The light at the top of the falls! I always wondered where it came from."

"The rainbow is only visible to a few," Laurel explained, "even though it is always there. It is only visible to the few Milohe has chosen."

119

Laurel made an easy dive straight down into the opening in the ground. At first Margaret thought they were diving right into the water, but then she realized there was plenty of clearance at the top of the opening for them to make it through without getting wet. Before she knew what was happening, they were flying straight down with the thundering falls underneath them. Margaret felt the delicious wet spray hit her face and she licked the water around her mouth eagerly. Then the swan evened off and they were level again, cruising just above the water. They passed over the quiet pool and Laurel turned to glance back at her.

"If on foot, as most landbred creatures are, there is an array of small steps that will take you down here to the left. Theodore chiseled them into the rock one summer and finds they are most convenient. They lead to a path that takes you the rest of the way. Of course, winging it by flying, in my opinion, is far more dramatic and much more efficient."

"Indeed," agreed Margaret. "I can't walk anymore, anyway. I suppose I shall just have to get around with you underneath me from now on. Will you be my wings, Laurel?"

"Of course," Laurel agreed readily. "But my legs are no good. As you know they waddle and they would look even more awkward on you than on me. Too short and too black. You wouldn't adjust well to the webbing between the toes. Besides, I doubt you would want to accompany me everywhere I go. I certainly would not do well in your schoolroom or at the dinner table."

"Laurel," Margaret asked tentatively, "would Joona water heal my back?"

"While you were in Joona you would be well," the swan said softly. "Able to run about like a gazelle. But because it is such a major injury, once you returned to earth all would revert back to the way it had been. Joona water loses some of its force once its healing power is taken from Joona to earth. Mild injuries it will sustain, but in your case, we must attempt a more permanent form of recovery."

"You mean I might be able to walk again?" Margaret asked eagerly. "Just like I used to? How could that happen?"

"Stranger things have been known to occur," Laurel responded softly.

Margaret didn't ask any more questions. She didn't want to know any more. She wondered if Milohe might have something to do with it all. She shuddered at the thought of meeting Him. It seemed so scary and uncertain. She didn't know how to imagine Milohe. Laurel had said He was more of a person than what she knew people to be. What that meant she wasn't sure.

"Here we are!" cheered Laurel, as they suddenly veered upward and burst from the wet dark cave into the irridescent purple of the rainbow. "Welcome to Joona once again, Princess Margaret!"

"Am I really a princess?" Margaret asked, grinning from ear to ear.

121

She heard the buoyant melody of the music and it filled her up inside, as it always did, the way nothing else could ever do. Far away she heard voices and knew that the swans were singing.

"I placed the wreath of woven vines on your head," Laurel reminded her. "Remember? Made for you and you alone by the swans, pruned from the archway that leads to Milohe himself. There can be no greater honor, Margaret. You are and always will be princess here."

They passed through gold, then crimson, and finally green. Margaret was glad to be back. She felt a sharp pain radiate down both arms and she stiffened. Below her she could see swans dotting the clear shining water like miniature sailboats stretched out to the horizon.

"Margaret!" shouted a familiar voice.

Margaret peered over Laurel's shoulder. Samson and Priscilla were waving their wing at her. It was Priscilla who had called.

"No star this time!" Margaret shouted down to them. "Otherwise I'd stop."

Samson and Priscilla nodded as they flew on. They came to a small gathering of swans by a pine tree. The swans raised their heads at Laurel's approach and recognized Margaret.

"Hey, it's Margaret!" someone called out. "Margaret, it's me, Hector!"

"Constantine, here!"

"And Evelyn!"

The swans were delighted to see Margaret, and

by the look in their eyes Margaret could tell they expected her to stop and visit.

"I can't stop now!" she yelled down to them as Laurel swooped lower. "I've got no star and I can't walk! We'll talk later."

They whizzed by and Laurel ascended again and entered the crimson band in the rainbow. The bright red band of color turned everything else around it crimson, even Laurel's feathers and Margaret's skin. Again Margaret felt her back spasm and she winced. This time Laurel knew. The swan must have felt her body tensing up.

"Do forgive me," Laurel intoned. "I am trying to fly as smoothly as I can, but air travel can be difficult on the passenger's back at times. Too much shifting back and forth. Motion discomfort I think they call it on the jumbo jets. I will try to slow down."

"It's not your fault," Margaret said, rather short of breath because of the pain. "You didn't do anything."

They flew for a while in silence. The crimson band had a quieting effect on Margaret. Her pain subsided and her expectation rose. She was about to enter the archway of light. She was about to see the very essence of Milohe. She breathed deeply. The next thing she knew, they were descending through a damp white mist and Laurel had found his footing on the diamond. As the mist cleared, a welcome breeze caressed Margaret's face. It smelled deliciously of pine and lilac.

As Margaret looked around, all was as she remembered it: the brilliant diamond reflecting the rainbow that arched above them with prisms of color; the grassy area surrounding the diamond which grew dark green pine trees and bushes laden with purple lilacs; the clear water on one side stretching out to the horizon. Margaret's eyes turned toward the little knoll. There, just as it had been before, stood a tall wide pillar of light. It stood erect and still. Inside the pillar the arched doorway hanging heavy with vines beckoned to her as it had done before. She longed to go through it.

"Oh Laurel," Margaret begged. "That entryway is calling to me, just like it did the first time I was here."

"It is time," Laurel responded kindly. "This time we shall go in together."

Laurel flew over to the knoll and stood at the outskirts of the archway.

"Hang on tightly, Margaret," he cautioned. "This can be turbulent at times."

Then, with a few determined strides forward, Laurel entered the arched doorway with Margaret, wide eyed and breathless, clinging to his neck for dear life.

9

MILOHE

Margaret had trouble describing what happened next when she tried to tell others later. She felt as though her brain wasn't big enough or there weren't enough letters in the alphabet to construct the words she needed to express it all. The best way she could explain the sensation she had after stepping into the pillar of light was that of being propelled backwards at an amazing speed. It was as if the light had her, and she, clutching to Laurel's feathery neck, was literally and completely at its mercy.

For those first moments, as she was being sucked backwards, Margaret felt weak and small in comparison to the tremendous pull all around her. It was like the pull of water upward when you dive down to the bottom of a pool. She was moving so rapidly, still astride Laurel's back, that it seemed as though very soon they were going to reach the end of something or the beginning of something and not be able to go any farther. The whole thing didn't last very long. Just as Margaret was beginning to get the feeling they were headed for a smash-up somewhere, they suddenly jolted to a stop and were plunked down.

At first Margaret couldn't tell where they were at all. The light was so bright she gave up trying to keep her eyes open. Slowly, after a little time had elapsed, she tried very carefully to open one eye just a tiny slit. She was still sitting on Laurel but he wasn't moving or saying anything, so she was very curious to know where they were. From what she could tell, the light was still bright, but for some reason, now it was tolerable. She opened her one eye all the way and then the other eye, blinking widely.

The air was fresh and clean, smelling of pine and lilac. She could see that they were outside somewhere on a little grassy slope looking up at a small hill. Margaret's eyes followed the line of the hill to the summit. What she saw there astounded her.

A large, golden throne loomed up from the summit of the hill and seated on the great throne was a most beautiful being. The being had a human face but it appeared to be made of bright white light, brighter than the sun. Margaret could not look directly at the face for very long. When she was able to look for short snatches (for there was something about the face that compelled her to look at it) the thing that struck Margaret the most about the face were the eyes. They were enormous.

Laughter and life brimmed up in them like dancing pools of water that seemed to hold all the colors of the rainbow in them at once. At the same time she noted in them an intense longing, and it seemed as if, surprisingly, the longing was for her. As she took quick snatches of the vast, penetrating eyes that seemed to want to draw her into them, Margaret felt the light, supple movement of the creature's heart in her own chest. It was an odd sensation and yet it warmed her whole being with the gentle yet persistent rhythm of movement and peace.

The being, whom Margaret knew immediately to be Milohe, actually reminded her of Laurel, although she did not know why. Perhaps it was the movement in his eyes. Perhaps it was the two pointed wings that shot up from behind his back and sparkled in the light like gleaming silver swords. The rest of Milohe was big, much too big to take in all at once. It would have taken Margaret forever to see every part of him, and the luminous quality of his face was so great that she found it difficult to move beyond the magnetic draw of his eyes.

Suddenly Margaret saw Milohe hold out a flaming sceptor to her. She knew the gesture was one of greeting and she bowed her head down low until it touched the base of Laurel's neck, for she was still on his back. It's not like she had thought of bowing down beforehand, or that anyone told her to. It was just a natural response to this being whose majesty filled the entire area with vibrating energy. Then he spoke. As he did so, Margaret let out a little gasp. His voice sounded exactly like the music of Joona that the rainbow played.

"Greetings!" he announced melodically. "I have been expecting you."

Margaret couldn't find her tongue, and her eyes remained glued to Laurel's back. She was grateful that Laurel said something.

"Milohe," Laurel responded in his most casual voice, "I have brought Margaret. As we both have discussed, she is in need of healing, not only here in Joona but in the dark recesses of the earth where she lives with other landbred creatures."

As Laurel spoke, his face looking up into Milohe's, Margaret gasped, not from fear but from the beauty of what was taking place. The radiance of color in Milohe's eyes that she had noticed before suddenly seemed to shoot out like glistening streamers. The streamers, which were really stripes of colored light, wrapped themselves loosely about Laurel as if in an embrace, and then flung themselves into the sky to form a brilliant rainbow. One end of the rainbow lay pulsing around the base of Milohe's throne. The other end was looped about Laurel's feet. The rainbow was vibrant and moving constantly, connecting the two of them in a kind of whirly dance. Each time either Milohe or Laurel spoke to the other one, the rainbow would shimmer and flex itself with a kind of rapturous ecstacy.

"Margaret," said Milohe, "is my favorite name.

There are many different kinds of healing, Margaret."

"Really?" Margaret asked, her voice trembling.

"Yes," Milohe declared, his eyes flashing more color at her. "Joona is deeply indebted to you, Margaret. Thank you for your great service, especially to the one they call Darcy."

"You're welcome," Margaret said, stammering a little bit. "I didn't think it was any big deal at the time."

Milohe actually laughed then. It was an easy kind of laugh, filled with the rich warmth of genuine surprise.

"How wonderful you are, Margaret," Milohe declared. "You really are fit to be the princess here."

"I certainly agree," Laurel chimed in. "We could tell when we chose her, Milohe, remember? She was so delightful."

The rainbow shimmered and bounced about.

"How could I forget?" Milohe said, reminiscing as if he were a proud parent. "Even the rainbow sang for us and promised her to us."

The response of the rainbow, after flexing and shooting off sparks of color, was to begin to play the music of Joona, softly and eagerly in the background.

Margaret couldn't believe it. It was like her meetings with Laurel and all her times in Joona had been planned from the beginning. It was so weird to think that even when she thought she had been doing her own thing, she actually had been doing their thing. Perhaps once she had become a follower of Laurel her thing and their thing had become one and the same. There was something safe about it all. It made her feel cared for.

"And now, Margaret," Milohe asked with great gentility, but also with extreme seriousness, "What would you have us do with the small one they call Sebastian? Would you have me destroy him?"

"Bring him out, Milohe," Laurel suggested. "Let us have a look."

Margaret realized then that the teamwork between Laurel and Milohe was quite equal. The functions of the two were different, but neither one seemed to be in control of the other. There was a deep understanding and friendship between the two of them that ran closer than blood, and the bond holding them together as unshakable as granite was expressed in the dancing radiance of the rainbow. She could see both of them in the other one's eyes. It was like seeing the same creature twice but in a different form altogether.

"All right," Milohe agreed.

He didn't summon Sebastian. Suddenly Sebastian was just there standing in front of Margaret on the little hill looking extremely green and thin. Margaret couldn't believe she had ever been afraid of him. Next to the brilliance of Milohe and the white blazing feathers of Laurel, he looked like a piece of parsley that someone pushes to the side of their dish in order to enjoy the main course. She couldn't see why he had ever dared to go against

Milohe, Laurel, and the Rainbow. What had possessed him to think he could win Joona from them? There, in the dark recesses of his cave, learning black magic and scheming day after day, Margaret decided, he must have gone a little bit insane. That's the only way she could begin to account for it.

"Well, Margaret?" Laurel asked her with majestic gravity. "Sebastian stands before you. What is your wish?"

Sebastian's eyes were like slits and he was staring at her viciously. His eyes glowed a ghastly green. Margaret wasn't sure if his eyes were squinty because the light was so bright, or if he was just trying to look fierce to scare her. Needless to say, he didn't intimidate her at all. Margaret realized that Milohe and Laurel were waiting for her to say something, so she cleared her throat in preparation, but her words got swallowed up and jumbled. Something inside her was holding back from lowering the final verdict. Something inside Margaret still wanted Sebastian to change his mind about things and become a friend, not a foe. She waited a few moments and then finally her voice seemed to return to her, so she asked him a question.

"Sebastian, how do you plead?"

Sebastian's neck shot upright and his eyes opened wide. He looked surprised. *Perhaps*, thought Margaret, *he thought she was intent upon destroying him as soon as she could.* Now he could be hoping for a second chance.

"I don't know what you mean," he declared flatly. "I am not pleading. Do you see me pleading? I am Sebastian, the great one, and I do not plead."

"You are on trial, Sebastian," Laurel told him firmly. "Thanks to Margaret's indulgence. All who are on trial are either guilty or not guilty. You are being asked to state which, in your opinion, you are."

"That just shows your simple-mindedness," Sebastian said with a superior edge to his voice. "You cannot be just guilty or not guilty. There are too many shades of gray and levels of meaning. Too many variables, too many questions and opinions. There cannot be some absolutely firm definition of 'guilty,' just as there cannot be an absolute definition of 'not guilty.' There is no way to answer your question with a simple word. It would take years and years to determine and evaluate the correct response to something as complex and uncertain as the meaning of 'guilty.'"

Margaret just stared at him, puzzled. She couldn't really understand what he was talking about.

"Are you saying that you don't think you did anything wrong?" she stammered uncertainly.

"Wrong?" Sebastian uttered with a low, gutteral growl. "I am not sure what you mean by wrong. It all becomes highly subjective when you start throwing these words around that mean one thing to one creature and quite something else to another. What I might do to wrong you might be a very good thing for me, you see. Who is the final judge, I ask, as to the 'rightness' and 'wrongness' of things? It is a highly speculative venture to propose an irrefutable standard of behavior on a species that is known for its broad wingspan and perspective."

Margaret was quiet. She didn't understand everything he was talking about and wondered if Sebastian knew what she meant by the word *wrong*. He certainly seemed to have his own ideas about what was wrong to serve his own purposes. *After all*, she mused, *he thought up all those punishments for the suffering swans' disobedience when he had possession of the castle*. He certainly didn't seem uncertain then about who was the final judge.

Suddenly the earth underneath them began to shake and tiny cracks appeared in the ground as if an earthquake were beginning. A voice like thunder bellowed down from the throne on the hill and white light flashed out all around them.

"We are the rightness of things!"

Milohe had issued a judgment. The ground shook again and his voice reverberated in her ears.

"Laurel, the rainbow, and myself. We are the rightness of things."

It was a judgment, thought Margaret, standing spellbound, not daring to move. It was a judgment, because if they were the rightness of things, then Sebastian was the wrongness of things—as wrong as wrong could be. As light flashed out from Milohe's throne, the area became even brighter and everything became much more distinct and brilliant. Even the green grass was silhouetted in a brilliant white hue. Sebastian, on the other hand, seemingly found it quite distasteful. His eyes were only open halfway now, and he was shading them with one wing.

"I say," he moaned. "Turn down the confounded lights."

The light intensified.

"Sebastian," Margaret asked, suddenly sensing that his time with them was short, "wouldn't you consider coming over to our side? Joona could be your home then."

"I am not satisfied to simply live in Joona," Sebastian countered, putting up his other wing for shading as well. "Other simpleminded souls may be, but not me. I am an idealist and I cannot deal with the mismanagement of space. This country is in need of complete . . . complete . . . over . . . haul. The present situation . . . is . . . chaotic and . . . unprecedented anywhere . . . else. . . ."

Sebastian's speech faltered and he crumpled to the ground. Margaret watched him collapse like a balloon until he was flat on his belly, his wings sprawled out on either side of him and the underside of his beak lying flat on the ground. His eyes were pinched tightly together in wrinkled lines.

"I say," Sebastian griped weakly, "turn down those confounded lights. They're killing me."

It was getting extremely bright now. Margaret knew that if the light continued to grow at its present pace, in a little while she would not be able to stand it either. She put up her hand to shield her eyes. It was then she saw that Sebastian had changed. He had begun to shrivel and was writhing about like a wriggling worm on blacktop. The light was not particularly hot. It was just bright. Brighter than the brightest white imaginable. It literally seemed to be killing him.

"There is still time, Sebastian," Laurel urged him. "If you would only change your mind!"

"No! No! No!" Sebastian rasped like a spoiled child. "I will not! This is my kingdom. My kingdom! Mine! Mine! Mine! Margaret is mine to destroy! Not yours! Mine, I say! Give her to me, I say, the filthy wretch. Give her to me!"

"The verdict, Margaret?" Milohe asked her, a certain urgency in his voice.

Margaret didn't answer right away because for a second Sebastian had actually frightened her. Even though his eyes were closed and he was flapping about on the ground like a half-drowned rat, his voice had a murderous, venomous quality to it, especially when he had said "filthy wretch." She remembered waiting for him to command the Leadership to throw her into the lake of sulfur as she stood in the haze of the sulfuric mist on the brink of extinction. The terror of it came sweeping back like a nightmare. Now when he said her name he growled it as if he wanted to sink his teeth into her neck and shake her unconscious. Margaret clung a bit closer to Laurel.

"Margaret," Laurel said patiently. "Don't be afraid. Nothing can harm you now. What is your verdict?"

"Guilty," she whispered softly.

The next minute Sebastian gave a wild shriek. He did this because the light flashing out from the throne suddenly intensified and the area they were standing in was completely taken up in a white brilliance that was as bold and powerful as lightning. In fact, the light seemed to be pulsating up and down as if it could hardly contain its own energy. The only thing that was not taken up in the white light was the rainbow, which also continued to grow brighter and brighter and pulse with color and life. Margaret noticed that Laurel was standing motionless looking straight up at Milohe. It seemed to her that Milohe was also looking straight at Laurel, although she couldn't be sure. She had to cover her eyes with her hands. It was far too intense of a light for her to endure for long.

Then Margaret heard a sizzling sound like bacon on a grill. Peering through her fingers she looked at where Sebastian had been. Nothing was there but a flat place in the grass. The grass itself had turned white in the light. Sebastian had evaporated into nothingness.

"I thought, perhaps, if we showed him our glory," Milohe's voice called out to Laurel, "he might give in."

"He didn't want to see it," Laurel said gravely.

"So it wasn't my fault?" Margaret asked relieved, her hands still over her eyes.

"Of course not," Laurel responded. "You simply stated the truth, which he in his own ignorance refused to see. The light revealed too much. He couldn't stand it. He fought it and it ate him alive. The only way to survive the light is to give yourself to it."

Margaret had her whole face buried in her hands now. Her head was bowed down low with her forehead resting against the base of Laurel's neck. She felt as if she were going to faint. The light was too bright even for her, and she didn't know how much longer she could endure it.

"Child," Milohe's voice called out with vitalizing buoyancy. "The fullness of time has come. I hearby grant you right of passage for as long as you reside in Joona. Anywhere you wish to go in Joona is yours to enjoy. You no longer need to wear the star, for you are no longer an alien but a resident. I grant your companions the same right of passage. Go in peace, and enjoy all things fully as they were meant to be enjoyed."

Margaret could see the light through her hands and she closed her eyelids. She felt herself hurtling forward and had to reach out and grab the base of Laurel's neck before she toppled off. The light was so bright that she cried out. She couldn't bear it and was sure now that she was not only a cripple but blinded as well. Clinging as she was to Laurel's neck with her eyes closed tight, Margaret could only guess that she had been taken by the light again and it was driving them forward at a million miles an hour. She cried out, for the light was searing and painful. As she did, she felt a warm rush down her spine. Then she heard a loud snapping. Margaret jolted upright. The bones in her back! They had come together and the pain was gone.

10
THE BANQUET

The ride through the light was fierce and awesome. Margaret never forgot the sensation. What had happened was engraved on her memory forever. She decided to leave it that way and not try to write about the experience like she usually did. A few blank pages in her journal served to mark the experience for her. On these pages she would never write a word.

The ride through the light lasted only a few moments before they came to a sudden stop. Margaret felt Laurel reach around with his long neck and nuzzle her knee with his beak.

"Come, Margaret," he said with mirth in his voice. "Open your eyes. You shall now see things that previously have been unseen by landbred creatures."

Margaret opened her eyes and recognized the place at once. They were standing in the throne room of the castle, and Joona music was playing. She could see the rainbow from the open windows and the fragrance of pine and lilac filled the air. Up on the platform was a golden throne, and beside it was another smaller throne. On the smaller throne lay her wreath of grape vines—her crown.

"You can climb off my back now," Laurel told her gently. "Milohe has granted your healing."

Margaret already knew that. Her spine felt straighter and stronger than it had ever been. Eagerly she jumped down from Laurel's back and stood next to him. She was grinning from ear to ear.

"Look at me Laurel!" she said, laughing. "Look at me!"

Laurel reached out his long slender neck and examined her carefully up and down.

"You look pretty sturdy," he agreed, bending down low in a swan smile. "Who told you that you couldn't walk, anyway?"

Margaret just grinned. She couldn't bring herself to do anything else. Then she noticed that everything in the room seemed uncommonly bright. The marble platform was glossy and shining, the rainbow out the window was splendorous and bold, the thrones were a dazzling gold.

"Laurel," she mustered, "everything is so . . . so beautiful."

"That is because Milohe has not only touched your back, he has opened your eyes as well."

When Laurel said this, the room seemed to fairly dance with light, and Margaret saw more.

In the center of the throne room was a long banquet table covered with food. The plates were a polished silver. The tablecloth was a thick blue tapestry embroidered with swans and rainbows and stars. In the center of the table stood three golden candles in silver holders. They were lit and their flames flickered in the fragrant breeze blowing in from the open windows.

Gathered around the table were faces of swans and of people she knew. The people were all looking at her and smiling. Even the swans were smiling with their bright eager eyes and the pleasant way they cocked their heads.

Margaret's gaze traveled swiftly from one face to the next. There was Uncle John and Wilda holding hands. Wilda was smiling and crying at the same time. Next to them stood Samson and Priscilla, Hector and Alexander. Then Margaret saw Darcy's face in the middle of a large crowd of swans. Behind her and off to one side, Casey and Beatrice stood with their stocky arms around each other. Ryan, Craig, and Heather were standing at one end of the table. Theodore was at the other end waving his big white hand at her.

"We've all come to the banquet!" Theodore called out. "All is now completed in the fullness of time. Let the festivities begin!"

The Joona music swelled. The swans joined in and the room was filled with song.

How beautiful the rainbow whose light
    reverses death!

How beautiful the great white swan whose
    death became our life!
How wonderful the children who led us out
    of fright!
As long as we live, we will thank you! Thank
    you! Thank you!

During the singing, Alexander got up from his
place and waddled over to the throne. Grabbing the
wreath of vines in his beak he brought it to Laurel,
who placed it carefully on Margaret's head just as
the words of the song were ending. Then everyone
broke out into a cheer.

"Long live princess Margaret! May she wear her
crown well!"

Margaret felt herself being swooped up in the
strong arms of her uncle.

"Oh Margaret!" he cried. "You are standing
again. You can walk! What greater miracle could I
ask for?"

Margaret looked at her uncle and saw him in a
way she had never seen him before. The lines in his
face seemed to have smoothed, his shoulders
weren't stooped, and his smile was wide and bold.

"Uncle John," Margaret gasped. "You look
different."

"I suppose I must be in love," he said mirthfully.

Margaret looked at Wilda who had followed him
over. She was still dabbing at her eyes with a han-
kie. Margaret blinked. Wilda looked younger too.
In fact, she looked gorgeous. The tiny strain lines at

the corners of her eyes were gone. Her hair was not slightly gray at the temples but a rich wavy brown. Margaret glanced at Laurel slightly confused. She didn't understand.

"You are seeing things," the swan explained gently, "the way they were meant to be. You are seeing things as they are in the fullness of time."

"Margaret," Wilda said, tears glistening on her cheeks. "I remembered it all once we got here. I was here before as a very young child. I must have been no older than three. I had gotten lost in the woods when my family took me on a picnic. I wandered around crying until I came to a pond. It was getting dark and I was scared. Your friend here, Laurel, brought me to Joona to spend the night. I rode on his back all the way. I remember the freshness of the air in my face and the freedom I felt. In the morning he dropped me off at my parents' door. They could never explain how I got there."

"I always thought you were one of Laurel's own," Margaret said, holding Wilda's hands and gazing into her eyes. "You had that certain look about you."

Craig, Ryan, and Heather came over and each of them gave her a warm embrace.

"Gee whiz, I'm so glad you're all right!" Ryan declared happily. "It's as if I'm in a dream."

"Sebastian is no more," Margaret told them. "I stood in the presence of Milohe, and Sebastian evaporated into the light."

"Evaporated?" Craig asked, astounded.

"Just what I said," Margaret told them. "Zap and he was gone like it was no big deal."

"So what is Milohe like?" asked Heather eagerly.

"He's wonderful. He reminds me so much of Laurel."

"We should have killed Sebastian the first time we saw him," Craig said regretfully. "Massacred him!"

Margaret looked at her three friends. Ryan was standing up straight and his hair was combed for once. He looked almost handsome. Heather, with her wild blond hair flying up around her face and her relaxed, gentle smile, looked like an angel. Craig was breathing through his nose, and his round, deep blue eyes were sparkling. She loved them more than she ever had.

"Gee whiz, Margaret," Ryan observed. "Your face, your whole self is so bright. Just like Laurel."

Something made Margaret look to her right. There stood Darcy by herself, looking longingly over at them.

"C'mon," said Margaret to the others.

She led the way over to Darcy's small, quivering form.

"Hi, Darcy!" Margaret said when she got to her. "Sit next to me at the table, won't you? Just like we do at school."

She pulled out a chair and Darcy sat down. Margaret sat down next to her, and Ryan flanked her on the other side.

"I wasn't sure you meant what you said in the

hospital room," Darcy said haltingly. "I don't see how you could ever forgive me."

"Darcy!" Margaret said, laughing. "You are my friend! This is now, and all is already forgiven. Life is lived in the present, Darcy. Don't miss this banquet! Look," she continued, reaching for a silver plate full of grape twizzlers and fruit candies, "all you can eat for free! Boy, if Clyde Thompson could only see us now!"

Darcy grinned and grabbed a twizzler. Margaret looked around the great company surrounding the long table. There were more swans there than she could ever remember seeing before.

"The princess has begun the meal," Theodore announced with a shout. "Let us join her in this great celebration. Sebastian is dead and our princess's coronation is a coronation for us all!"

"Hurray!" shouted all the swans and people together.

Then they began to eat. The food was succulent and deliciously seasoned. There seemed to be everybody's favorite food available. Even the swans had various types of seaweed they could munch on along with some other green varieties of things that Margaret had no idea what they were.

"How did all of you get here?" Margaret asked suddenly above the hum of conversation and laughter in the room.

She hadn't even thought of it before. It had all seemed so natural to have everyone together.

"Theodore brought us," Casey announced.

He had been quiet up to this point, and Margaret looked up and smiled at him. He nodded to her.

"Your uncle convinced me to go with him. I never would have come otherwise. Thought this whole thing was a pipe dream. Reckon I was wrong."

"I'll say," Beatrice echoed, munching on a peanut butter sandwich—her favorite.

"We went down through the falls," Theodore added. "It's the best way to come on foot."

"A rather long walk, if I must say so," Beatrice said, wincing a little. "I think I might have lost a few pounds on the way. Much worth it once we got here though."

Someone dinged a spoon on the side of a goblet. Everyone stopped talking and looked up. It was Laurel. He was standing at one end of the table with the spoon in his beak. Laying the spoon on the table he bent down low in a swan smile.

"I am so glad you could come to our banquet," he stated heartily to them all. "Especially the land-bred creatures who are with us for the first time. Please do not eat like the birds. This meal was prepared with the human anatomy in mind and we assumed you would come with hearty appetites."

His tone was polite and regal as if he were addressing distinguished celebrities.

"Milohe and I prepared it for each of you. We have long wanted you landbred creatures as our guests but had to wait for the fullness of time. Here it is. Things as they were meant to be. I formally declare that Margaret Morrison is now princess of Joona and shall reign in Joona for as long as she is meant to reign. We have crossed the time barrier on our journey through the light. When each of you children return to earth you will simply pick up where you left off. There will be no time lost on earth as was the case formerly.

"Adults, I fear that you have lived too long to be exempt from earth's timing. You must return shortly. Your visit here will, however, bless your life on earth with tremendous fruit. You shall go about your days with the blessing of Milohe, the rainbow, and myself hovering about you.

"Finally, children, you must decide who you shall be while you are here in Joona. You may be anything you desire. Joona is yours to dwell in, not as strangers but as residents. Also, you may be granted one wish for your life on earth, which shall return to you one day."

"I know what I want to wish for," blurted Heather. "I wish that we did not have to move away from our hometown and that my father's farm would succeed and we'd have plenty to live on. And oh, Laurel, I want to spend my days in Joona flying on Alexander. He and I are great pals. We had such a lively blast last time we were here."

"Granted," said Laurel pleasantly. "We have need of a messenger here. Someone who can disperse news quickly across the great expanse of Joona. A carrier swan, Alexander! That is what you shall be, and carry Heather on your back with all the news to the far ends of our country."

Alexander bowed down low and looked extremely honored. Laurel looked around him for a moment with his great dark eyes, and finally his gaze rested on Darcy.

"What about you?"

Darcy looked over at Laurel, surprised.

"Me?" she exclaimed. "Why me?"

"I said all the children had wishes," Laurel said sincerely. "And you are what landbred creatures call a child, are you not?"

"You mean I shall stay here too?" Darcy asked, amazement written over her face.

"As long as you are meant to stay," Laurel assured her.

"Then I guess what I want most is to be Margaret's servant and friend," Darcy declared haltingly. "She saved my life. Whenever she needs me I want to be there for her. I want to serve her as long as I live."

"Granted," Laurel assured her. "The hatching of a new beginning, which will be beneficial for you both."

Margaret reached over and embraced Darcy.

"You shall only be my friend, Darcy," she whispered. "Never my servant."

"For me," uttered Craig, not waiting to be asked, "I think I'd like to learn how to swim while I'm here. Perhaps I could look for buried treasure in the water. And as for earth, well, it would be nice to be able to breathe through my nose."

Everyone cheered their agreement.

"Granted," said Laurel kindly.

Craig was sitting next to him and Laurel reached over and jabbed him affectionately with his beak.

"Ryan, it's your turn," Laurel said.

"Gee whiz," Ryan murmured a bit uncertainly. "I suppose I might like to build a small hospital."

"What do you mean?" Heather exclaimed. "There's no need for a hospital here."

"Hospitals are awful," Margaret shuddered. "Heather's right."

"But sometimes they can be really good. What about a sort of recovery rehabilitation hospital for the suffering swans when they first arrive? You know, one that's bright and airy and beautiful. Some of the swans are in pretty tough shape. They might need a place to settle down and rest and be cared for at first. What about it, Laurel?"

"A wonderful idea." Laurel thought about it, his eyes bright. "We could definitely find a suitable place for such a fledgling facility. It would give the suffering swans a real boost when they first come. And for earth?"

"That I shall one day become as good a doctor as John Morrison who was there for my mother when she needed him most."

John's eyes were teary. He wiped them and mouthed a thank-you across the table to Ryan.

"Granted," Laurel declared. "There is no doctor better than John Morrison."

There was a brief pause as all eyes turned toward Margaret. She sat at the table, her head bowed low in thought. Laurel also turned and gazed at her with affection brimming in his eyes. Finally he summoned her quietly.

"And now, Margaret? What about you?"

Margaret raised her head, a soft smile forming at the corners of her mouth. Looking around at all of them she felt a tremendous surge of well-being.

"Well, I am princess, and that is what I most want to do while I am here. I want to wear this crown worthily and rule in peace. As for earth, I guess I'd like the swinging bridge to come back and last forever. May our children's children find it as magical and wonderful as we did."

"Granted," Laurel said happily. "A most honorable request and well worth the effort on my part to see that it is accomplished. The rest of you landbred creatures are adults and must forgo specific wishes, as these are designated only for the young. Still, you have eaten of the bounty of Joona and it is within my power to wish for you a continuation of the bounty you have experienced here at this table."

With this, Laurel raised both pearl-white wings and held them out over the heads of those who sat at the table. His voice was deep and majestic as he spoke, rumbling with the wisdom of eternity.

"May you each find your lives on earth full of fruit, celebration, and love. May your eyes be turned toward the invisible that lasts rather than the visible which soon perishes. May you sense the reality of impossibility in your life and find Milohe's blessing at every turn."

A deep hush settled on the group and Laurel's blessing hung like rich perfume in the air, sifting down its moist fragrance on all of them. Then the door to the banquet room breezed open. Everyone stood to their feet. A commotion ran through the crowd and someone whispered, "It's the queen."

Margaret's mother entered. She saw Laurel and bowed low. She was dressed in flowing blue robes that reminded Margaret of the blue waters of Joona. As she rose, she smiled and held her arms out to Margaret. Margaret ran to her and they embraced.

"Well, I'll be," muttered Casey under his breath. "Stranger than strange if you ask me."

Uncle John was at Margaret's side in a moment.

"Annie," he gasped. "You're alive!"

The queen embraced John as well. Then she turned back to Margaret.

"There is someone else I would like you to meet, Margaret," she said with joy spilling out of her eyes.

The door opened and in strode a man. His eyes were sparkling and he sported a wide moustache that turned up at the ends. Margaret recognized him at once from the picture John had given her. It was her father.

"Meet your daughter, Grant," said the queen, gesturing toward Margaret.

"Margaret!" exclaimed Grant with delight. "I have waited so long for this day."

He knelt down and embraced her. Margaret's heart was full. She loved her father instantly. To feel his strong embrace and his moustache scratch her cheek when he kissed her was more than she could take in. They were together again! All of them. This was her family.

"Laurel found me," Grant explained. "I had lost my way and was wandering in the land of the shadows. He found me and brought me here. I never dreamed it would be as wonderful as this. It's so very bright and colorful."

Margaret looked around to find Laurel. He had disappeared.

"Don't worry, Margaret," piped Alexander. "He was called away just seconds ago. He's a free bird, but he will return. He always does, you know."

"I know," said Margaret, glancing gratefully at Alexander. "You can't keep him just for yourself. He belongs to everyone."

"Come, Margaret," her mother said, taking her hand. "Take your rightful place next to me on your throne."

Thus began the reign of Margaret Morrison in Joona. Margaret and her parents dwelt there in peace for many years. Margaret grew to be a stunning young woman. She wore long royal robes, but she always wore her hair in braids. She preferred it that way. Ryan built his hospital and many a swan recovered there in the beauty and serenity of its walls. Craig learned to swim as well as any swan in Joona. Heather became Joona's messenger and was heralded as the best swan rider in all the country. She even learned to ride Alexander when he did four acrobatic flips in the air in succession. As for Darcy, she became Margaret's bosom friend. There was nothing Darcy wouldn't do for Margaret and nothing Margaret could not tell her.

None of them could even fathom the idea of going back to earth, although sometimes Margaret did get a bit lonely for Uncle John. Earth seemed so dark and dismal compared to the glory of Joona.

11
THE SWAN BOAT

One day when the children were all together on the banks of Joona's clear sparkling water, Ryan spotted a large ship in the distance with wide white sails and a wooden bow. On one of the sails was imprinted a large colorful swan.

"Whatever could that be?" Margaret asked.

"It's the swan ship!" Heather cried excitedly. "I've heard about it in my travels across Joona. It's an enchanted boat that everyone wants a chance to ride on. It will bring all kinds of good fortune, and it only appears once in a great while."

They jumped up and down on the beach heralding the boat. To their delight, it turned and started toward them. In his eagerness Craig swam out halfway to meet it.

"C'mon!" he cried out excitedly after he had

climbed on board. "There's no one here. This ship must be directed by magic!"

By now the ship was fairly close to the shore and the others came in after him.

"I wonder where it will take us," Darcy asked Margaret, as she climbed up the rope ladder that hung from the ship's side. "Perhaps to the very end of Joona itself."

As soon as they were aboard the ship took off. At first they seemed to be following the rainbow. Then they turned a corner and the rainbow disappeared.

"I've never been in these parts before," Heather remarked.

The pine trees were thinning out now and the water looked murky. The ship pulled up along the shore. They were surrounded by weeping willows and maples. White iron benches lined the shore. Suddenly the ship stopped.

"Where are we?" Ryan asked.

"I've been here before," Darcy declared. "Yes, I know that I've been here before."

"The park!" Margaret half-screamed.

Suddenly she looked down at herself. She was no longer wearing the rich robes of a princess. Instead, she had on her faded trusty overalls from years ago.

"Why, we're back!" Craig shouted. "It's the park by the school. The way we walk home sometimes. And, hey, you guys. My nose is still clear."

"Do you suppose, Margaret," asked Ryan seriously, "that my mother and your uncle have married yet?"

"Laurel said we weren't supposed to lose any time here," Margaret reminded him.

"Oh, yeah," said Ryan. "That seems like ages ago."

They scrambled down from the boat and slogged up the bank. When they made it to dry ground they all charged off in different directions. Despite the glory of Joona, they had all missed their families and couldn't wait to see them again.

When Margaret got home, Uncle John was standing on the front porch.

"Hi, Margaret," he said casually. "I just returned from Joona. Wasn't the banquet wonderful?"

"Uncle John!" Margaret cried out. "I've missed you terribly."

"Oh, I see," John said, embracing his niece and smiling. "You've been gone from me a lot longer than I've been gone from you, I suppose. C'mon in, Margaret. I'll make you some cocoa and you tell me all about it."

Margaret lived with Uncle John for many years after that. She grew up all over again, got married to a kind man who looked a great deal like her father, and had a little boy and a little girl of her own. She named them Christopher and Julie. Margaret and her husband never left Uncle John's quiet town. They both loved the woods too much, the river, and yes, the new swinging bridge that wasn't quite so new anymore. Darcy's mother had the town replace it a year after she had insisted it be torn down. She did it out of gratitude to Margaret for saving Darcy's life. People thought Mary Lupus had gone insane when she offered to pay for the construction of the new bridge herself as long as the town agreed to pay for its upkeep. No one had any objections, however.

←←←

One beautiful day as Margaret took a walk through the woods, she decided to take the long way home past the bridge. As the bridge came into view, something white caught her eye. She looked over and saw an enormous white swan floating in the water. She looked again and saw that the swan had its neck bent low in a smile. However, he was not smiling at her. She followed the swan's gaze and saw that he was smiling at a little boy and girl. There was her own Christopher and Julie standing at the water's edge.

"Greetings, Christopher," the swan declared merrily. "Greetings, Julie, my dear."

"Hello," said Christopher, taking a step closer. "How did you know our names?"

Margaret watched as the swan paddled closer to her children.

"I know you both quite well," the swan told them. "Would you like a ride on my back?"

Both children nodded eagerly. "Do you have a name?" asked Julie wonderingly.

With a glance backwards, Margaret slipped off into the woods. She didn't want to bother them. The last thing she saw was her children astride the great swan's back, their eyes bright with anticipation.

158

Be sure not to miss any of these exciting NavPress fiction titles!

Journey to Joona (THE JOONA TRILOGY, Book 1)
Kim Engelmann (#0-89109-865-8)

Defenders of Joona (THE JOONA TRILOGY, Book 2)
Kim Engelmann (#0-89109-866-6)

The Crown of Joona (THE JOONA TRILOGY, Book 3)
Kim Engelmann (#0-89109-867-4)

The Secret of the Mezuzah
Mary Reeves Bell (#0-89109-872-0)

Treasure in an Oatmeal Box
Ken Gire (#0-89109-367-2)